THE HEALING BREATH

Life force is contained in the breath that we breath. Altered states of awareness and profound healing are possible with just using the breath. Scientists have found that just 15 minutes of deep breathing can give us all the energy we need for the day.

The Healing Breath describes the numerous benefits that simple breathing techniques can bring us, e.g., proper breathing, pranayama, yoga breathing, colour breathing, etc.

LUIS S.R. VAS

The Healing Breath

Breathing Techniques for Better Health

New Age Books

New Delhi (India)

THE HEALING BREATH

ISBN: 978-81-7822-164-9

Reprint: Delhi, **2018**
First Indian Edition: Delhi, 2004

Published by
NEW AGE BOOKS
A-44 Naraina Industrial Area, Phase-I
New Delhi (India) - 110 028
E-mail: nab@newagebooksindia.com
Website: www.newagebooksindia.com

Library of Congress Cataloging-in-Publication Data
Vas, Luis S.R.
ISBN 978-81-7822-164-9
Includes Glossary, Index
Health/Yoga

Printed and published by
RP Jain for NAB Printing Unit
A-44, Naraina Industrial Area
Phase-I, New Delhi-110028. India

Preface

For thousands of years spiritual seekers, mystics and yogis have realized the innate spiritual quality of the breath. If we stop breathing for just a few minutes we are dead. Life force is therefore contained in the breath that we breathe. Yogis for ages have used the powers of breath to transform consciousness; indeed a psycho-spiritual reaction takes place with the use of these breathing techniques.

Altered states of awareness and profound healing are possible with just using the breath. Today we are privileged to have teachers to instruct us on the proper use of the breath for these purposes.

Scientists have done research on things that give us lots of energy to do all we need to do to go from "rags to riches" physically, mentally and spiritually. Of all these things, from coffee to ginseng to artificial stimulants to working out, they found that just 15 minutes of deep breathing can give us all the energy we need for the day.

In this book, we cover the numerous benefits that simple breathing techniques, which are described here, can bring us.

Luis S.R. Vas
vasluis@hotmail.com

Contents

CHAPTER 1

Benefits of Proper Breathing

Proper breathing has profound effects on our health. Over 70% of waste by-products are eliminated through our breathing and our skin. When our blood is heavily oxygenated it becomes very difficult for viruses and bacteria to grow in our body. Good breathing supports muscle growth and energy to get things done. Very often our "breathing mechanism" is in need of healing as a result of the breathing trauma we sustained at birth. The umbilical cord was probably cut too soon for many of us. Our first breath was filled with fluid, painful, scary and the result of being hit! Whenever we undergo difficult moments in life now we tend to hold our breath. This then shuts down the musculature of the whole "mechanism", creating body armour, thus locking in place the tension of the difficult moment. Moments begin to pile up like this and soon we are only using 20% of our capacity to breathe, thus having only 20% of our energy capacity.

Anatomy of Breathing

In normal respiration the air is taken in through the nostrils without any special effort, sound or exaggerated movement of the nose or chest. In short, it is done unconsciously. We are not even aware of air traveling through our nostrils, down the nasal and oral parts of the pharynx, of its reaching the larynx and then the trachea and the lungs. In general, most of us are unaware of how the breathing process works.

Here we will take a look at:

- Stages in breathing
- Kinds of breathing
- Organs of breathing
- Processes in breathing, and
- Ways of controlling breathing.

Stages in Breathing

Each single act of normal, unmodified breathing consists of four distinguishable stages:

- "Breathing In", Inhaling or Inspiration.
- The Pause, Short or Long, between Inhalation and Exhalation. We will call this Retentive Pause and readjustment phase.
- "Breathing Out," Exhaling or Expiration.
- The Pause, Long or Short, between Exhalation and Inhalation. We will call this stage Extensive Pause and its readjustment phase.

The two "resting" stages may or may not be very restful since the whole respiratory system, including its muscular and nervous mechanisms, undergoes a reversal of direction and multitudes of minute adaptations take place whenever each such reversal occurs.

All four are entailed in a complete act of respiration.

Kinds of Breathing

We can distinguish at least 11 different kinds of breathing. These are given below.

Although yogic treatises do not normally do so, J.M. Dechanet, author of 'Christian Yoga,' identifies two ways of breathing: "One for men, the other for women". He says that a woman's breathing rhythm is more rapid than a man's and that her upper chest expands first, whereas a man's breathing rhythm is slower and his abdominal expansion comes first. Although, doubtless, physiological differences in men and women do affect their breathing, I suspect that the world over, women breathe more placidly than men and that the differences which Dechanet notices may be related partly to size of body rather than sex. Smaller bodies may be expected to have a shorter, and perhaps more rapid, rhythm stroke than larger bodies. The fact that women live longer than men, on the average, may be due to many factors; but a study of breathing habits in men and women, especially in the older ages, may prove enlightening. However, distinctions of sex do not normally play a significant role in discussions of breathing.

1. Noisy versus quiet breathing is a distinction which has its significance in other conditions. Snoring may indicate deep slumber; wheezing, asthma and panting, shortness of breath; and other noises, clogging of nasal passages. But traditional yogic exercises do deliberately seek to control the loudness or softness of breathing and, in addition to giving directions for increasing loudness and softness, often combine both increases and decreases in subtle ways, synthesizing them in larger, more encompassing experiences, as in mantric chanting of the sacred symbol om.
2. Fast and Slow Breathing
3. Regular and Irregular Breathing
4. Jerky and Smooth Breathing
5. Deep and Shallow Breathing
6. Forced and Effortless Breathing
7. Voluntary and Involuntary Breathing
8. Mouth and Nose Breathing
9. The distinction between "high," "middle," and "low" breathing, where most of the expansion is

in the top, middle or bottom parts of the chest and lungs, and the joining of all three in "complete yogic breathing".

10. The distinction between the mere passage of air in and out of lungs (with related physiological and mental effects) versus experiencing breathing as an affair of the whole body, the whole self, even of the whole universe as explored in pranayama.
11. The distinction between nervous and relaxed, vs. anxious and peaceful, breathing.

As we can see from the above classification of various breathing types, the process of breathing is very complex.

Organs of Breathing

Our respiratory system consists of nose and mouth, pharynx and larynx, trachea and bronchi, lungs and thorax.

Nose and Mouth

The nose consists of an outer shape and skin (which often receives more attention), and two air passages (nostrils).

Your nostrils differ in size and shape from those of other people. Most people breathe primarily through one nostril more than another. Whether relatively long or short, large or small, straight or crooked, nostrils vary in circumference and contour throughout their length. The bottom or floor surfaces of the nostrils tend to be more horizontal and the top or roof surfaces have been shaped more like an arch. A bony and cartilaginous septum separates your two nostrils.

The several nasal sinuses, including the better-known frontal sinuses in the forehead above the eyes and the maxillary sinuses on each side of the nose, play various roles in breathing, thinking, illness and in yoga. Most of us realize their existence when they become infected, as with colds, hay fever, or noxious gases or dusts, resulting in headaches. Some sinuses appear to perform an important function in cooling the brain. Nervous activity uses energy which seems to generate heat that needs to be conducted away. Thus, somewhat like the radiator of an automobile, the sinuses may serve as a cooling system for the brain, which supplements the circulatory system wherein the blood serves as a coolant. We seem to be able to think better when we have a "clearer head" resulting from well-ventilated sinuses. Deep breathing and posture exercises not only increase oxygenation through the lungs and circulation of the blood within the brain, but also tend to enlarge and clear the sinus cavities for freer air circulation.

The skin lining the nostrils consists primarily of membranes which do not dry out easily in the presence of moving air. They are kept moist by secretions called mucus which sometimes dries and hardens into a cake which must be expelled. Hairs embedded in such membranes, especially near the outer opening, often grow into sieve-like mats which catch and repel small objects, insects and dust. Olfactory end-organs are embedded in these membranes and some areas have a thick, spongy tissue which expands, so much sometimes—especially when irritated by infections or allergies—that it closes the nostril completely. Although yogic exercises may be insufficient by themselves to relieve clogged nasal conditions, they may help considerably.

The mouth, too, is an important air passage—especially when we need more air than can be forced through the nostrils, as when we gasp for air or pant or puff, and when the nostrils are closed by swollen membranes or mucous discharge. Membranes lining the mouth and tongue seem to dry up from air movements more rapidly than nasal membranes though saliva aids in maintaining moistness. The oral passage may be closed by the lips, by the tongue pressed against the teeth or roof of the mouth, and sometimes with the aid of the soft palate. Directions for opening and closure, partial or complete, of the mouth constitute parts of some directions for traditional yogic exercises.

Pharynx and Larynx

The pharynx is the opening behind the nasal cavities and mouth. It is bounded by the root of the tongue and is lined with tissues called tonsils which may become enlarged partially obstructing the passage of food and air. Two Eustachian tubes, which permit adjustment of atmospheric pressure in your middle ears, open from the sides of the pharynx. The pharynx ends in the esophagus or tube leading to the stomach and the larynx or "voice box," which contains the vocal cords and glottis and muscles needed for producing sounds. A cartilaginous epiglottis at the top of the larynx aids in closing it tightly so that solid and liquid foods will not be permitted to enter it during swallowing. Respiration is interrupted during swallowing. Yogis sometimes deliberately hold the epiglottis aperture closed to force holding air in or out of the lungs in certain exercises.

Trachea and Bronchi

The trachea or "windpipe" is a tube kept open against pressures because its walls consist in part of cartilaginous rings, or semi-rings. It is lined with a mucous membrane containing hair-like cells which beat upward toward the nose and mouth and move mucus and the entangled dust particles in that direction. It ends by dividing into two other tubes called bronchi which in turn branch again and again until they terminate in bronchioles, thin-walled tubes which lead to tiny air sacs with their small dilations called alveoli where most of the gas exchange takes place.

Lungs and Thorax

Each of the two lungs consists of—

- Bunches of bronchioles and alveoli
- Blood vessels and capillaries, and
- Elastic tissue.

These are arranged in lobes and are surrounded by a membrane that secretes a lubricating fluid. The lungs, together with the heart, occupy most of the thoracic or chest cavity, bounded on the sides by the ribs and on the bottom by the diaphragm. The diaphragm separates the chest cavity from the abdomen containing most of the digestive system.

The pleural sacs and the inner lining of the thorax are airtight. Since the only opening from the outside is the trachea, air may be forced in or out of the lungs by enlarging or compressing the thoracic area. Three sets of muscles are primarily responsible for changing the size of the thorax. These are:

- Those acting on the ribs
- Those acting between the ribs, and
- Those acting on the diaphragm.

Other muscles of the body, such as those in the arms, legs and back, may twist the body so as to distort its usual shape and exert pressures that squeeze or expand the chest cavity. A blow on the abdomen, wearing tight clothes, a full stomach or intestinal gas may also provide temporary pressures on the thorax thus affecting the breathing process.

Processes in Breathing

Respiration

An average adult at rest inhales and exhales about sixteen times per minute. Each time, half a litre (about a pint) of air is drawn in and expelled. At the end of a normal expiration, one may force out an additional litre and a half of air, leaving about an additional litre in the lungs which cannot be forced out. Also, after normal inspiration, one may inspire an additional one and a half litres. So it is possible to increase the amount of air inspired and expired during each breath from half a litre to three and a half litres.

Not all of the air breathed can be used by the body because some must remain to fill the nose or mouth, sinuses, larynx, trachea, bronchi and their larger branches. This is the "dead air" in contrast with "alveolar air" which participates in gas exchange. The shallower the breathing, the larger becomes the percentage of dead air in each breath. But also, in shallow breathing, more impurities are retained.

Most breathing exercises in yoga have the effect of increasing both the amount and percentage of air which enters actively into the purifying gaseous exchange processes.

The air inhaled normally consists of about 79% nitrogen, about 20% to 21% oxygen, about 0.04% carbon dioxide, with traces of other gases and water vapour. Exhaled air often consists of about 79% nitrogen, about 16% oxygen, about 4% carbon dioxide, with traces of other gases and water vapour. Since the nitrogen content remains approximately the same the most significant change during the breathing process is an exchange of about 4% oxygen for about 4% carbon dioxide.

Oxygenation

When the percentage of oxygen exchanged for carbon dioxide remains the same, the total amount of oxygen and carbon dioxide exchanged per minute tends to increase as a greater air volume is breathed. One may, by strenuous exercise, increase the volume of ventilation to ten times the resting level. Or one may deliberately force increased ventilation without exercise. When muscular exercise increases, the body needs more oxygen. When ventilation is forced intentionally, some increase in oxygen content and decrease in carbon dioxide content of the alveoli and blood may be expected. Part of the aim of both deep breathing exercises and posture movements and rests is to "purify" (increase the ratio of oxygen to carbon dioxide) the blood and the various parts of the body through which blood circulates.

The interchange of oxygen and carbon dioxide is possible because of the structure of the cells joining the alveoli and the capillaries and the laws and processes of gas exchange. The movement of carbon dioxide from the blood to the alveoli takes place by diffusion. In diffusion, the carbon dioxide moves from the rich side to the lean side. When the blood contains more carbon dioxide than the air, the carbon dioxide will diffuse from the blood to the air. If, on the other hand, the air is rich in carbon dioxide, the diffusion of carbon dioxide from the blood to the air is inhibited. In extreme cases the carbon dioxide may even diffuse or flow from the air into the blood. Thus, our breathing habits are very important.

Regulation

A group of nerve cells in the medulla, the respiratory centre of the brain, controls the contractions of muscles used in breathing. Inspiration takes place when the nerve cells of this group send impulses through motor nerves to respiratory muscles. When something, we do not know what, prevents these cells from sending impulses, inspiration ceases and expiration occurs. Apparently we do not use muscular energy and force to expel air but merely stop inhaling; then exhaling takes place automatically, without muscular effort. Since all respiratory muscles contract in a harmonious way, some organizing process in the brain marvellously coordinates their movements. Apparently, the respiratory centre cells function much like the pacemaker tissue of the heart, since they seem to induce rhythmic patterns of respiration without outside help, even though they are sensitive to various influences which modify their action.

In addition to the involuntary regulation and regularization of breathing patterns, many involuntary reflexes also exist, such as those noticeable in choking, sneezing, coughing, and swallowing. It is almost impossible to breathe while swallowing food. Other reflexes may be noted, such as sudden holding of breath when you sniff ammonia and similar chemicals. If your air supply has been cut off, you automatically gasp for breath. Emotional excitement, fear, anger, enthusiasm all stimulate breathing, as may sudden increase in either heat or cold.

There is voluntary control of breathing. For example, you can deliberately take a deeper breath or stop breathing momentarily. Such direct control may be supplemented by indirect intentional control, as when we dance or kiss or drink or smoke or sing. We may deliberately run for such a distance that we get our "second wind," after which we breathe more easily even though exercising strenuously.

Part of the significance of distinguishing between voluntary and involuntary control of breathing is that yogic exercises aim first at changing unhealthy involuntary patterns voluntarily and then at an establishment of more healthy patterns. Whereas nervous tension produces some inhibiting influence upon deep, regular breathing patterns, deliberate effort to counteract these influences in such a way that our more completely spontaneous and uninhibited rhythmic patterns become restored as needed.

From now on we will consider ways of controlling breathing and their benefits.

Chapter 2

Pranayama: The Breathing Exercises of Yoga

Pranayama, as traditionally conceived, involves much more than merely breathing for relaxation. Pranayama is a term with a wide range of meanings. Patanjali defines pranayama as "the regulation of the incoming and outgoing flow of breath with retention". It is to be practised only after perfection in asana is attained. Pranayama also denotes cosmic power, or the power of the entire universe which manifests itself as conscious living being in us through the phenomenon of breathing.

The word pranayama consists of two parts: prana and ayama. Ayama means stretch, extension, expansion, length, breadth, regulation, prolongation, restraint and control and describes the action of pranayama. Prana is energy, when the self-energizing force embraces the body. When this self-energizing force embraces the body with extension, expansion and control, it is pranayama.

Prana

Prana is an auto-energizing force which creates a magnetic field in the form of the Universe and plays with it, both to maintain, and to destroy for further creation. It permeates each individual as well as the Universe at all levels. It acts as physical energy, mental energy, where the mind gathers information; and as intellectual energy, where information is examined and filtered. Prana also acts as sexual energy, spiritual energy and cosmic energy. All that vibrates in this Universe is prana: heat, light, gravity, magnetism, vigour, power, vitality, electricity, life and spirit are all forms of prana. It is the cosmic personality, potent in all beings and non-beings. It is the prime mover of all activity. It is the wealth of life.

This self-energizing force is the principle of life and consciousness. It is the creation of all beings in the Universe. All beings are born through it and live by it. When they die, their individual breath dissolves into the cosmic breath. Prana is not only the hub of the wheel of life, but also of yoga. Everything is established in it. It permeates life, creating the sun, the moon, the clouds, the wind, the rain, the earth and all forms of matter. It is both being (*sat*) and non-being (*asat*). Each and every thing, or being, including man, takes shelter under it. Prana is the fundamental energy and the source of all knowledge.

Prana and Consciousness (*Citta*)

Prana and citta are in constant contact with each other. They are like twins. Prana become focused where citta is, and citta, where prana is. Yoga suggests that as long as the breath is still, prana is still, and hence citta is still. All types of vibrations and fluctuations come to a standstill when prana and citta are steady and silent.

Because of this connection between breath and consciousness, yoga has devised pranayama to stabilize energy and consciousness.

With reference to yoga prana can be described as something that flows continuously from somewhere inside us, filling us and keeping us alive: it is vitality. In this image, the prana streams out from the centre through the whole body. Pranayama is the measuring, control, and directing of the breath, and thus of energy within the organism, in order to restore and maintain health and to promote evolution.

When you are troubled, restless, or confused, you have more prana outside the body than within. When you feel unwell; the quality of prana and its density within the body is reduced. Too little prana in the body can be expressed as a feeling of being stuck or restricted. It can also show as a lack of drive or motivation to do anything; you are listless or even depressed. We may suffer from physical ailments when prana is lacking in the body. Yoga Sutra mentions disturbances in the breath, which can take very different forms. On the other hand, the more peaceful and well-balanced we are, the less our prana is dispersed outside the body. And if all the prana is within the body, we are free of these symptoms.

If prana does not find sufficient room in the body there can be only one reason: it is being forced out by something that really does not belong there—such as blockages caused by rubbish. When we practise pranayama, we try to reduce this rubbish and replace it with more and more prana within the body.

Our state of mind is closely linked to the quality of prana within. The more content a person is and the better he or she feels, the more prana is inside. The more disturbed a person is, the more prana is dissipated and lost. Because we can influence the flow of prana through the flow of our breath, the quality of our breath influences our state of mind and vice versa. In yoga we are trying to make use of these connections so that prana concentrates and can freely flow within us. One definition of the word yogi is "one whose prana is all within his body". In pranayama we want to reduce the amount of prana outside the body until there is none leaking out.

Prana is power. Proper acts of breathing are ways of harnessing that power. It gives control of breathing processes and control of vital force. Even though, in breathing, fresh air from outside the body enters the body and foul air leaves, mystical pranayama conceives appropriation of power as a bringing to conscious manifestation an omnipresent cosmic power which exists already latent within oneself as a particular expression of cosmic being. When a person attains a feeling of oneness with the rest of the universe, his anxiety tends to disappear. When the in-flowing breath is neutralized or joined with the out-flowing breath, then perfect relaxation and balance of body activities are realized. In yoga, we are concerned with balancing the flows of vital forces, then directing them inward to the chakra system and upward to the crown chakra or thousand petalled lotus (*sahasara*). When one acquires an intuitive apprehension of ultimate power and of one's own identity with it, one loses one's fear of external powers and develops a trust which is conducive to confident living.

Whatever happens in the mind influences the breath; the breath becomes quicker when we are excited and deeper and quieter when we relax. In order to influence our prana we must be able to influence the mind. Our actions often disturb the mind, causing prana to exude from the body. Through daily pranayama practice we reverse this process, as a change in the breathing pattern influences the mind.

The idea of prana existing within or beyond the body can be understood as a symbol for our state of mind. When the mind is as clear as transparent glass there is nothing that could disturb the body; there is no rubbish lying about. On the other hand, if we notice hesitancy, discontent, fear of doing something because it might be inappropriate, and so forth, we can assume that there are blockages in the system. These blockages do not just occur in the physical body; they exist even more in the mind, in consciousness. Every kind of rubbish we find in ourselves was originally produced by incorrect knowledge.

The link between mind and breath is most significant. The Yoga Sutra says that when we practise pranayama the veil is gradually drawn away from the mind and there is growing clarity. The mind becomes ready for deep meditations. Thus, pranayama is first and foremost awareness of the breath. Here, we focus our attention on the breath.

Without prana there is no life. We can imagine that prana flows into us as we inhale, but prana is also the power behind breathing out. As well, prana is transformed in the body into various powers, and is involved in processes that ensure that we rid ourselves of what we no longer need. Out breath is a very important part of the body's elimination processes. We can use out breath as a mechanism to free the mind from blocks and thereby lead us to greater clarity.

Pranayama or breathing technique is very important in yoga. It goes hand in hand with the asana or pose. In the Yoga Sutras, the practices of pranayama and asana are considered to be the highest form of purification and self-discipline for the mind and the body, respectively. The practices produce the actual physical sensation of heat, called tapas, or the inner fire of purification. It is taught that this heat is part of the process of purifying the nadis, or subtle nerve channels of the body. This allows a more healthful state to be experienced and allows the mind to become more calm.

In pranayama, we focus our attention on the breath. In the practice of pranayama, it is therefore very important to keep an alert mind, for the processes that are being observed are very subtle. There is no visible movement of the body as in asana practice; we must acutely sense and feel the movement of the breath within. The only dynamic process is breathing. Patanjali makes a few practical suggestions for keeping our attention on the breath. For example, we can focus on a place in the body where we can feel or hear the breath. Or we can try to follow the movement of the breath in the body, feeling the inhalation from the centre of the collarbone, down through the rib cage to the diaphragm, and following the exhalation upward from the abdomen. Another means for paying attention to the breath is to feel where it enters and leaves the body at the nostrils. It is also possible to listen to the breath, especially if you make a slight noise by gently contracting the vocal chords, a pranayama technique known as *ujjayi*.

Suggestions like these help us keep our attention on the breath and prevent our practice from becoming merely mechanical. The goal of pranayama is not to bring the inhalation and exhalation into a certain relationship with each other, or to establish a particular length of breath. If exercises such as these help us concentrate on our pranayama, that is wonderful. But the true aim of the various techniques and breath ratios of breathing in pranayama is first and foremost to give us many different possibilities for following the breath. When we follow the breath, the mind will be drawn into the activities of the breath. In this way, pranayama prepares us for the stillness of meditation.

The breath relates directly to the mind and to our prana, but we should not therefore imagine that as we inhale, prana simply flows into us. This is not the case. Prana enters the body in the moment when there is a positive change in the mind. Of course, our state of mind does not alter with every in-breath or outbreath; change occurs over a long period of time. If we are practising pranayama and notice a change of mind, then prana has long before entered the body. Changes of mind can be observed primarily in our relationships with other people. Relationships are the real test of whether we actually understand ourselves better.

The Forms of Prana

There are five forms of prana. They have different names according to the bodily functions with which they correspond. These forms of prana are:

- *udana-vayu,* corresponding to the throat region and the function of speech.
- *prana-vayu,* corresponding to the chest region.
- *samana-vayu,* corresponding to the central region of the body and the function of digestion.
- *apana-vayu,* corresponding to the region of the lower abdomen and the function of elimination.
- *vyana-vayu,* corresponding to the distribution of energy into all areas of the body.

Vayu is a sanskrit term meaning "air" or "breath". We will look at two of these forms: prana-vayu and apana-vayu.

Prana and Apana

That which enters the body is called prana and that which leaves it is called apana. The term apana also refers to the region of the lower abdomen and all the activities that take place there. Apana describes that part of prana that has the function of elimination and provides the energy for it, and it also refers to the lower belly and the rubbish that collects there when the power of prana is not in a state of equilibrium. When a person is slow and heavy we sometimes say that he has too much apana. Apana as pranic energy is something we need, but apana as refuse left from activating this energy actually prevents prana from developing within. All forms of prana are necessary, but to be effective they must be in a state of balance with each other. If someone has a lot of rubbish in the region of the lower abdomen then he or she consumes too much energy there, and this imbalance should be addressed. The goal is to reduce apana to an efficient minimum.

Apana as waste matter accumulates because of many factors, some of which lie within our control. The practice of yoga aims to reduce these impurities. People who are short of breath, cannot hold their breath, or cannot exhale slowly are seen as having more apana, whereas those who have good breath control are considered to have less apana. An overabundance of apana leads to problems in all areas of the body. We have to reduce the apana so that we can bring more prana into the body.

When we inhale, prana from outside the body is brought within. During inhalation, prana meets apana. During exhalation, the apana within the body moves toward the prana. Pranayama is the movement of the prana toward the apana and the movement of the apana toward the prana. Similarly, holding the breath after inhalation moves the prana toward the apana and holds it there. Holding the breath after exhalation moves the apana toward the prana.

Agni, the Fire of Life

What happens within this movement of prana and apana? According to yoga we have a fire, agni, in the body, situated in the vicinity of the navel, between the prana-vayu and the apana-vayu. The flame itself is constantly changing direction: on inhalation the breath moves toward the belly, causing a draft that directs the flame downward like in a fireplace; during exhalation the draft moves the flame in the opposite direction, bringing with it the just-burned waste matter. It is not enough to burn the rubbish; we must also rid the body of it. A breathing pattern where the exhalation is twice as long as the inhalation is aimed at providing more time during exhalation for freeing the body of its blockages. Everything we do to reduce the rubbish in the body is a step in the direction of releasing our blockages. With the next inhalation we bring the flame back to the apana. If all the previously burned waste has not left the body, the flame will lose some of its power.

Certain physical positions are beneficial for the meeting of fire and rubbish. In all inverted postures, the agni is directed toward the apana. This is the reason yoga attributes so much significance to the cleansing effects of inverted postures. Cleansing is intensified when we combine inverted postures with pranayama techniques.

All aspects of pranayama work together to rid the body of apana so that prana can find more room within. In the moment when waste is released, prana fills the space in the body where it really belongs. Prana has its own movement; it cannot be controlled. What we can do is create the conditions in which prana may enter the body and permeate it.

The beauty of prana is that through this, we can influence purusa, the essence of life. Yoga suggests that we can influence prana via our breath and mind. By working with these through pranayama, we create optimal conditions for the prana to flow freely within.

The Retained-breath Exercise

Physiologists claim that the air breathed in should remain in the lungs for ten to twenty seconds to maximize the gaseous interchange in the lungs. The yoga practitioners devised an exercise in which the breath is retained for four times the duration of inhalation (about twelve to sixteen seconds) thousands of years ago. Yogis and pranayama followers claim that this exercise would take maximum advantage of the air inhaled.

Benefits

1. It provides the optimum supply of oxygen to the body. Even jogging and other aerobic exercise

doesn't achieve this, since the breathing is quick and shallow and there is no retention of oxygen.

2. The air which has remained in the lungs from previous inhalations is purified.
3. There is increased oxygenation of the blood.
4. The retained breath gathers up some of the waste matter of the body and expels it on exhalation.
5. The lungs increase their elasticity and capacity and become more powerful. This allows benefits to be enjoyed all day, not just during the exercise.
6. The exercise builds a bigger, more powerful chest and prevent, or helps to correct sagging breasts in women.

Technique

1. Sit up straight.
2. Inhale for four seconds. Push your stomach forwards to a count of two seconds and then push

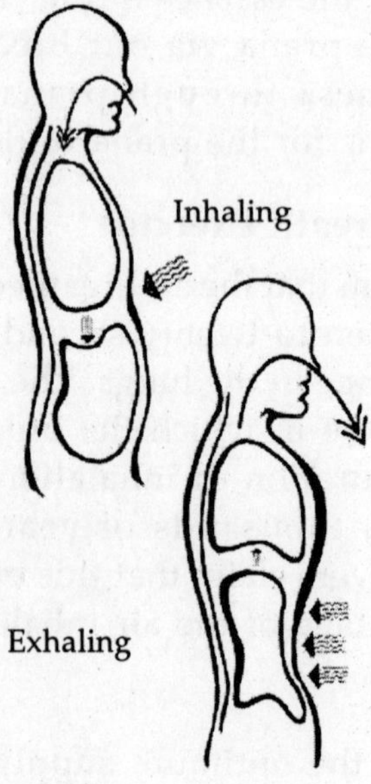

Fig. The retained-breath exercise

your ribs sideways for one second, and finally lift your chest and collar bone upwards for one second. This makes a total of four seconds.

3. Hold the breath for sixteen seconds. If you find this is difficult at the start, just hold for eight seconds, and gradually over a period of a few months build up to sixteen seconds.
4. Exhale for eight seconds. For the first six seconds, just allow the collar bone and ribs to relax, so the breath goes out automatically. For the last two seconds push the stomach in gently to expel the air from the lungs.

Do this exercise only once the first week, and add one more round each week, until you are doing three rounds.

The yogi rule for the retention breath is that exhalation should be twice that of inhalation, and retention should be four times that of inhalation; that is, a ratio of 1:4:2.

Use visualization as with the rhythmic breathing exercise for added benefits.

CHAPTER 3

Yoga Breathing Research

"Yoga breathing through a particular nostril increases spatial memory scores without lateralized effects," by Naveen K.V.; Nagarathna R.; Nagendra H.R.; Telles S., of the Vivekananda Kendra Yoga Research Foundation, Bangalore, India, in *Psychol Rep*, 1997 Oct, 81:2, 555-61.

Abstract

Uninostril breathing facilitates the performance on spatial and verbal cognitive tasks, said to be right and left brain functions, respectively. Since hemispheric memory functions are also known to be lateralized, the present study assessed the effects of uninostril breathing on the performance in verbal and spatial memory tests. School children (N = 108 whose ages ranged from 10 to 17 years) were randomly assigned to four groups. Each group practised a specific yoga breathing technique: (*i*) right nostril breathing, (*ii*) left nostril breathing, (*iii*) alternate nostril breathing, or (*iv*) breath awareness without manipulation of nostrils. These techniques were practised for 10 days. Verbal and spatial memory was assessed initially and after 10 days. An age-matched control group of 27 were similarly assessed. All four trained groups showed a significant increase in spatial test scores at retest, but the control group showed no change. Average increase in spatial memory scores for the trained groups was 84%. It appears yoga breathing increases spatial rather than verbal scores, without a lateralized effect.

"Pranayama increases grip strength without lateralized effects," Raghuraj P.; Nagarathna R.; Nagendra H.R.; Telles S. of the Vivekananda Kendra Yoga Research Foundation, Bangalore, India, in the *Indian J. Physiol Pharmacol*, 1997 Apr, 41:2, 129-33.

Abstract

The present study was conducted to determine whether breathing through a particular nostril has a lateralized effect on hand grip strength. 130 right-hand dominant, school children between 11 and 18 years of age were randomly assigned to 5 groups. Each group had a specific yoga practice in addition to the regular program for a 10-day yoga camp. The practices were: (1) right-, (2) left-, (3) alternate-nostril breathing, (4) breath awareness and (5) practice of mudras. Hand grip strength of both hands was assessed initially and at the end of 10 days for all 5 groups. The right-, left- and alternate-nostril breathing groups had a significant increase in grip strength of both hands, ranging from 4.1% to 6.5%, at the end of the camp though without any lateralization effect. The breath awareness and mudra groups showed no change.

Hence, the present results suggest that yoga breathing through a particular nostril, or through alternate nostrils increases hand grip strength of both hands without lateralization.

CHAPTER 4

Colour Breathing

Colour breathing is a form of meditation or visualization, in which you imagine yourself inhaling and exhaling colours. It can be practised in bed before going to sleep, or when waking in the morning.

1. Find somewhere comfortable to sit or lie down and relax.
2. Keep your breathing deep, regular, and calm.
3. Breathe rhythmically from twelve to eighteen times a minute. If possible, use the colour of the spectrum or its nearest equivalent. Imagine the self engulfed by a white light that enters through the head from the cosmos down to the extremities and floods the entire organism from within and from without. Keep this image for two minutes.
4. Imagine yourself surrounded by intense light of the colour you choose. Be aware of the healing properties of the light.

Red, yellow and orange, whichever one is used, is visualized as being drawn up from the earth through the soles of the feet to the various organs. The length of time for visualizing the red part of the spectrum is two minutes.

Blue, violet, and indigo should be visualized as coming down from the atmosphere as vertical rays into the anterior fontanel to the various organs. The length of time for visualizing colours in the blue part of the spectrum is three to four minutes.

Green should be visualized as coming into the navel on the horizontal plane. The length of time for visualizing the colour green is one minute in a waving motion upward from the umbilical cord and one minute downward from the umbilical cord, but always on a horizontal plane.

5. As you breathe in, imagine that you are inhaling this colour, and follow it as it spreads from your lungs to your solar plexus and then throughout your body as discussed for each color.

6. As you breathe out, imagine that you are exhaling the complementary colour.

7. Now mentally bathe the body and allow the entire self to be engulfed in a white light for two minutes.

CHAPTER 5

Breathwork Therapy

This modality uses a combination of techniques which allow one to release both the physical trauma and emotional trauma from the "breathing mechanism". Once cleared, we are freed on a new level that opens us to lots of love, joy and energy. Below are a few of the many techniques that are used along with others.

These techniques only require 15 minutes a day. Three are shared here.

Three-part Breath

This is the easiest and the most profound, can be done anywhere at any time.

1. Comfortable seated or standing, take a deep breath into the abdomen, through the nose, so that it expands out like a balloon.

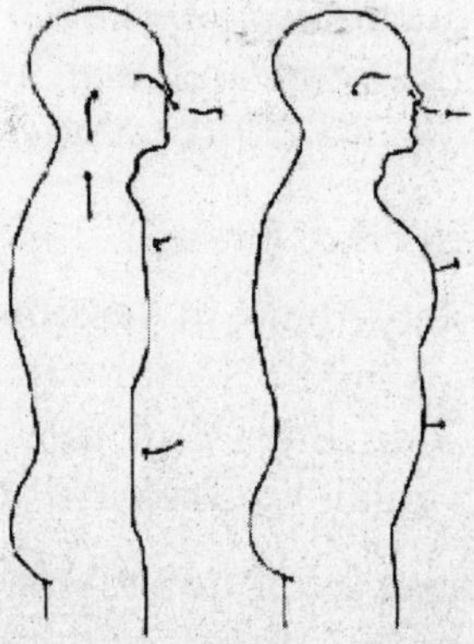

Fig. Three-part breath

2. Next continue the inhale to now expand the ribcage with air.
3. Next continue the inhale further to now expand the chest all the way to the upper chest, like a balloon.

Then reverse the procedure by exhaling out first from the chest, then the ribcage, then the abdomen.

Pulling in on the abdominal muscles at the end of the exhale, getting out all the air. Then reverse the process by breathing in again. Imagine that your torso is a glass and that the glass fills up from the bottom to the top and then empties from the top down to the bottom. Do this for up to 15 minutes.

Bellows Breath

This is great for charging up with energy or to release stress.

1. Best if seated and not driving. Spine straight.
2. Imagine that you are blowing a piece of dust out of your nose by sharply pulling in on the abdomen and at the same time blowing air out the nose.
3. Relax and a natural inhalation will occur to fill the lungs again.
4. Again, sharply blow air out the nose by pulling in on the abdomen. Continue with the cycle so that your abdomen is functioning like a bellows, blowing air out.
5. Do this for 22 cycles and then stop and take a big breath and rest. Do three rounds of 22.

Conscious Connected Breath

This is used by Rebirthers in sessions. It has profound healing and transformational qualities when done properly with a Rebirther. Can safely be done on own for short times to relax and release stress.

1. Only to be done lying down and for just 15 minutes. Further use of this breath requires the guidance of a trained Rebirther.

2. Begin with a full inhalation into the chest through the mouth.
3. Without pausing or holding, immediately allow the exhalation to gush out of the mouth without pushing it or holding it back. A simple relaxed exhalation.
4. Then without pause begin the inhale again, pulling air up into the chest.
5. Continue with a relaxed exhalation as soon as the inhalation stops.

This is also called the circular connected breath. Meaning that it has no pausing in it at all, but is one continuous loop.

Chapter 6

Importance of Breathing

Breathing is important for two reasons. It is the only means to supply our bodies and its various organs with the supply of oxygen which is vital for our survival. The second function of breathing is that it is one means to get rid of waste products and toxins from the body.

Why is Oxygen so vital?

Oxygen is the most vital nutrient for our bodies. It is essential for the integrity of the brain, nerves, glands and internal organs. We can do without food for weeks and without water for days, but without oxygen, we will die within a few minutes. If the brain does not gets proper supply of this essential nutrient, it will result in the degradation of all vital organs in the body.

The brain requires more oxygen than any other organ. If it doesn't get enough, the result is mental sluggishness, negative thoughts and depression and, eventually, vision and hearing decline. Old people and those whose arteries are clogged often become senile and vague because oxygen to the brain is reduced. They get irritated very quickly.

Poor oxygen supply affects all parts of the body. The oxygen supply is reduced to all parts of the body as we get older due to poor lifestyle. Many people need reading glasses and suffer hearing decline in old age.

When an acute circulation blockage deprives the heart of oxygen, a heart attack is the result. If this occurs to the brain, the result is a stroke.

For a long time, lack of oxygen has been considered a major cause of cancer. Even as far back as 1947, work done in Germany showed that when oxygen was withdrawn, normal body cells could turn into cancer cells.

Similar research has been done with heart disease. It showed that lack of oxygen is a major cause of heart disease, stroke and cancer. The work done at Baylor University in the USA has shown that you can reverse arterial disease in monkeys by infusing oxygen into the diseased arteries.

Thus, oxygen is very critical to our well-being, and any effort to increase the supply of oxygen to our body and especially to the brain will pay rich dividends. Yogis realized the vital importance of an adequate oxygen supply thousands of years ago. They developed and perfected various breathing techniques. These breathing exercises are particularly important for people who have sedentary jobs and spend most of the day in offices. Their brains are oxygen starved and their bodies are just 'getting by'. They feel tired, nervous and irritable and are not very productive. On top of that, they sleep badly at night, so they get a bad start to the next day continuing the cycle. This situation also lowers their immune system, making them susceptible to catching colds, flu and other 'bugs'.

Oxygen Purifies the Blood Stream

One of the major secrets of vitality and rejuvenation is a purified blood stream. The quickest and most effective way to purify the blood stream is by taking in extra supplies of oxygen from the air we breathe. The breathing exercises described here are the most effective methods ever devised for saturating the blood with extra oxygen.

Oxygen burn up the waste products (toxins) in the body, as well as recharging the body's batteries (the solar plexus). In fact, most of our energy requirements come not from food but from the air we breathe.

By purifying the blood stream, every part of the body benefits, as well as the mind. Your complexion will become clearer and brighter and wrinkles will begin to fade away. In short, rejuvenation will start to occur.

Medical Science Verifies Oxygen's Importance

Scientists have discovered that the chemical basis of energy production in the body is a chemical called Adenosine Triphosphate (ATP). If something goes wrong with the production of ATP, the result is lowered vitality, disease and premature ageing.

Scientists have also discovered that oxygen is critical for the production of ATP; in fact, it is its most vital component.

Yoga permits us to tap into this vital nutrient.

Importance of Healthy Breathing

We know how to breathe. It is something that occurs to us automatically, spontaneously, naturally. We are breathing even when we are not aware of it. So it seems foolish to think that one can be told how to breathe. Yet, one's breathing becomes modified and restricted in various ways, not just momentarily, but habitually. We develop unhealthy habits without being aware of it. We tend to assume positions (slouched positions) that diminishes lung capacities and take shortened breaths. We also live in social conditions that are not good for the health of our respiratory system.

As discussed above, scientists have known for a long time that there exists a strong connection between respiration and mental states. Improper breathing produces diminished mental ability. The corollary is true also. It is known that mental tensions produce restricted breathing.

A normally sedentary person, when confronted with a perplexing problem, tends to lean forward, draw his arms together, and bend his head down. All these body postures result in reduced lung capacity. The more intense the concentration, the more tense the muscles become. The muscles in the arms, neck and chest contract. The muscles that move the thorax and control inhalation and muscular tenseness clamp down and restrict the exhalation. The breaths become shorter and shorter. After an extended period of intense focusing, the whole system seems to be frozen in a certain posture.

We become fatigued from the decreased circulation of the blood and from the decreased availability of oxygen for the blood because we have almost stopped breathing. As our duties, responsibilities and their attendant problems become more demanding, we develop habits of forgetting to breathe.

Try an experiment suggested by Swami Vishnudevananda. Focus attention upon the ticks of a clock placed at a distance of about twelve feet. If you get distracted, try concentrating harder until you experience the ticking with undivided attention. If you fail at first, you should try again and again until you succeed in keeping the ticking clearly in mind for at least a few seconds. What happened? The majority of persons who took part in this experiment reported that they have completely suspended the breath. The others, who had less concentration, reported that they experienced very slow breathing. This experiment shows clearly that where there is concentration of the mind, the breathing becomes very slow or may even get suspended temporarily.

What's wrong with the way we breathe?

Our breathing is too shallow and too quick. We are not taking in sufficient oxygen and we are not eliminating sufficient carbon dioxide. As a result, our bodies are oxygen starved, and a toxic build-up occurs. Every cell in the body requires oxygen and our level of vitality is just a product of the health of all the cells.

Shallow breathing does not exercise the lungs enough, so they lose some of their function, causing a further reduction in vitality.

Animals which breathe slowly live the longest; the elephant is a good example.

We need to breathe more slowly and deeply. Quick shallow breathing results in oxygen starvation which leads to reduced vitality, premature ageing, poor immune system and a myriad other factors.

Why is our breath fast and shallow?

There are several reasons for this. The major reasons are:

1. We are in a hurry most of the time. Our movements and breathing follow this pattern.
2. The increasing stress of modern living makes us breathe more quickly and less deeply.
3. We get too emotional too easily. We get excited easily, angry easily, and most of the rest of the time we suffer from anxiety due to worry. These negative emotional states affect the rate of breathing, causing it to be fast and shallow.
4. Modern technology and automation reduces our need for physical activity. There is less need to breathe deeply, so we develop the shallow breathing habit.
5. We are working indoors more and more. This increases our exposure to pollution. As a result, the

body instinctively inhales less air to protect itself from pollution. The body just takes in enough air to tick over.

As we go through life, these bad breathing habits we picked up become part of our life. Unless we do something to reverse these habits, we can suffer permanent problems. The good news is that these are reversible. The bad news is that before we can change these habits, we should recognize and accept that our behaviour needs to be changed. This means that we see for ourselves the benefits of good breathing techniques.

Certainly, yoga is not the only way to cope with the stress and the resultant drop in oxygen supply to the brain brought on by the constricted breathing. A coffee break, a trip to the restroom or a good laugh may all result in some readjustment of constricted breathing patterns. These can be thought of as "mini-yogas". We can benefit by taking or seeking more breaks, trips or jokes. But for those whose occupations continue to be highly stressful, something more will be needed. Deep breathing exercises and stretching of muscles, especially those primarily concerned with controlling inhaling and exhaling, should be sought. Participation in active sports also will be useful. Going for a walk is very good. Those experiencing restricted breathing at night, should actively pursue morning exercises.

The Effects of Shallow Breathing

1. Reduced vitality, since oxygen is essential for the production of energy in the body.
2. Increased disease. Our resistance to disease is reduced, since oxygen is essential for healthy cells. This means we catch more colds and develop other ailments more easily. Lack of sufficient oxygen to the cells is a major contributing factor in cancer, heart disease and strokes.

With our 'normal' sedentary way of living, we only use about one tenth of our total lung capacity. This is sufficient to survive, but not sufficient for a high vitality level, long life and high resistance to disease.

The ancient yogis knew the importance of correct breathing and developed techniques not only to increase health and life span, but also to attain superconscious states.

The Medical Viewpoint on Fast, Shallow Breathing

Modern science agrees with the ancient yogis on the subject of shallow breathing. An editorial in the Journal of the Royal Society of Medicine suggested that fast, shallow breathing can cause fatigue, sleep disorders, anxiety, stomach upsets, heart bum, gas, muscle cramps, dizziness, visual problems, chest pain and heart palpitations.

Scientists have also found that a lot of people who believe they have heart disease are really suffering from improper breathing.

Importance of Breathing through the Nose

The first rule for correct breathing is that we should breathe through the nose. This may seem obvious, but many people breathe principally through the mouth. Mouth breathing can adversely affect the development of the thyroid gland. It can retard the mental development of children.

The nose has various defence mechanisms to prevent impurities and excessively cold air entering the body. At the entrance to the nose, a screen of hairs traps dust, tiny insects and other particles that may injure the lungs if you breathe through the mouth. After the entrance of the nose, there is a long winding passage lined with mucus membranes, where excessively cool air is warmed and very fine dust particles that escaped the hair screen are caught. Next, in the inner nose are glands which fight off any bacilli which have slipped through the other defences. The inner nose also contains the olfactory organ—our sense of smell. This detects any poisonous gases around that may injure our health.

The yogis believe that the olfactory organ has another function: the absorption of prana from the air. If you breathe through the mouth all the time, as many people do, you are cheating yourself of all this free energy *(prana).* The yogis say this is a major factor in lowered resistance to disease and impairs the functioning of your vital glands and nervous system. Add to this the fact that pathogens can enter the lungs via mouth breathing, and you can see that it's impossible to be healthy, not to mention vital, if you breathe through the mouth.

It is easy to break the habit of breathing through the mouth. Just keep your mouth closed and you will automatically breathe through your nose!

Summary: Benefits of Deep Breathing

We will now summarize the benefits of deep breathing. Deep breathing produces the following benefits:

1. Improvement in the quality of the blood due to its increased oxygenation in the lungs. This aids in the elimination of toxins from the system.
2. Increase in the digestion and assimilation of food. The digestive organs such as the stomach receive more oxygen, and hence operates more efficiently. The digestion is further enhanced by the fact that the food is oxygenated more.
3. Improvement in the health of the nervous system, including the brain, spinal cord, nerve centres and nerves. This is due again to the increased oxygenation and hence nourishment of the nervous system. This improves the health of the whole body,

since the nervous system communicates to all parts of the body.

4. Rejuvenation of the glands, especially the pituitary and pineal glands. The brain has a special affinity for oxygen, requiring three times more oxygen than does the rest of the body. This has far-reaching effects on our well being.
5. Rejuvenation of the skin. The skin becomes smoother and a reduction of facial wrinkles occurs.
6. The movements of the diaphragm during the deep breathing exercise massage the abdominal organs—the stomach, small intestine, liver and pancreas. The upper movement of the diaphragm also massages the heart. This stimulates the blood circulation in these organs.
7. The lungs become healthy and powerful, a good insurance against respiratory problems.
8. Deep, slow, yoga breathing reduces the work load for the heart. The result is a more efficient, stronger heart that operates better and lasts longer. It also mean reduced blood pressure and less heart disease.

The yoga breathing exercises reduce the work load on the heart in two ways. Firstly, deep breathing leads to more efficient lungs, which means more oxygen is brought into contact with blood sent to the lungs by the heart. So, the heart doesn't have to work as hard to deliver oxygen to the tissues. Secondly, deep breathing leads to a greater pressure differential in the lungs, which leads to an increase in the circulation, thus resting the heart a little.

9. Deep, slow breathing assists in weight control. If you are overweight, the extra oxygen burns up the excess fat more efficiently. If you are underweight, the extra oxygen feeds the starving tissues and

glands. In other words, yoga tends to produce the ideal weight for you.

10. Relaxation of the mind and body. Slow, deep, rhythmic breathing causes a reflex stimulation of the parasympathetic nervous system, which results in a reduction in the heart rate and relaxation of the muscles. These two factors cause a reflex relaxation of the mind, since the mind and body are very interdependent. In addition, oxygenation of the brain tends to normalize brain function, reducing excessive anxiety levels.

The breathing exercises cause an increase in the elasticity of the lungs and rib cage. This creates an increased breathing capacity all day, not just during the actual exercise period. This means all the above benefits also occur all day.

CHAPTER 7

Learning to Breathe Correctly

We do deep breathing while asleep. Hence, a simple way to learn how to breath properly is to simulate sleep. Lie down, close your eyes, relax the whole body, drop the chin and imagine that you are asleep, thus letting your breathing become deeper and deeper.

In Yoga deep breathing, you start filling the lower part of the lungs first, then you fill the middle and upper part. When exhaling you first empty the upper part of the lungs, then the middle, and last of all the lower part.

This process, however, is not divided into three separate actions. Inhalation is done in one smooth continuous flow just as one might pour water in filling a glass. First the bottom is filled, then the middle, and finally the upper portion. But the process itself is an uninterrupted one. Inhalation should be done in one continuous operation both the inhalation and the exhalation. Do it slowly and in a most relaxed manner. No effort or strain should ever be exerted. This is very important. Keep mouth closed.

You then become aware of the function of your own diaphragm. You expand the flanks when inhaling and contract them when exhaling. The lower part of the rib cage naturally expands first when you breathe in and is compressed last when you let the air out. This too should be done gently, without any force or strain. The chest remains passive during the entire process of respiration. Only the ribs expand during inhalation and contract during exhalation, accordion-fashion. To use force during inhalation is completely wrong. One should do it with ease, without any tension or strain whatever. In deep breathing, exhalation is as important as inhalation because it eliminates poisonous matter. The lower part of our lungs seldom are sufficiently emptied, and tend to accumulate air saturated with waste products, for with ordinary breathing we never expel enough of the carbon dioxide our system throws off even if we do inhale enough oxygen. If, on the other hand, the lower part of the lungs are properly expanded and contracted, the circulation in the liver and spleen, which are thus "massaged" by the diaphragm, are greatly benefited.

Inhaling

First, push the stomach forwards as you breathe in.

Second, push the ribs sideways while still breathing in. The stomach will automatically go inwards slightly.

Third, lift the chest and collar bone up while still breathing in.

Even though this is described as three separate processes, it should be done in a smooth, continuous rhythm with each part following smoothly on from the previous part. Try to avoid any jerky movements.

Exhaling

First, just allow the collar bone, chest and ribs to relax-the air will go out automatically.

Second, when all the air seems to be out, push the stomach in slightly to expel any remaining air in the lungs.

Exhaling is a more passive affair, except for the second stage when the stomach is pushed in slightly.

Basic Instructions for the Breathing Exercises

1. Find a quiet place where you won't be distracted. If doing the exercises inside, make sure the window is open to allow plenty of fresh air into the room.

2. Sit on a chair or if you prefer, cross-legged on the floor. Sit straight. Unless your spine is erect, some of the benefits of the breathing exercises will be lost.
3. Breathe deeply and slowly, without strain.
4. You should do the exercises on an empty stomach. Wait at least three hours after a heavy meal, and about one and a half hours after a light snack, such as fruit. There are two reasons for this. First, a heavy meal will reduce your concentration. Second, food in the stomach causes some of your blood and oxygen supply to be diverted to the stomach for digestion. This will reduce the blood and oxygen available for directing to the brain while you are doing the breathing exercises.
5. To gain maximum benefit, do the exercises twice a day, in the early morning before breakfast, and in the early evening. It's best not to eat for about fifteen minutes after the exercises.

While doing deep breathing the spine should be kept straight, so as not to impair the free flow of the life-force, or prana. This also helps to develop correct posture. The yogis attach such great importance to correct posture that they have devised several different positions for their various advanced breathing practices as well as for meditation and concentration. One very popular pose for deep breathing is lotus posture or cross legged posture.

When you sit down on the floor with your legs crossed, visualize a stream running through you in a straight line, starting at the top of your head and continuing into the ground. Imagine, too, that this is the axis around which your body has been moulded. This will help you learn to sit up straight without being stiff and tense. You should, in fact, feel comfortable and relaxed as you sit this way.

CHAPTER 8

Your First Deep Breath

Deep breathing can be accomplished sitting down in a meditative posture such as lotus posture, sitting down on a chair with your spine straight or standing up with your spine held straight. If you haven't done so, read the chapter on learning to breath correctly.

Fig. A meditative posture

First check your posture. The spine should be straight, the head erect, hands on knees, mouth closed. Now concentrate on the pharyngeal space at the back wall of your mouth and, slightly contracting its muscles, begin to draw in the air through that space as if you were using a suction pump. Do it slowly and steadily, letting the pumping sound be clearly heard. Don't use the nostrils; remember that they remain inactive during the entire respiration process. When inhaling let your ribs expand sideways like an accordion-beginning with the lower ones, of course. Remember, the chest and shoulders should remain motionless. The entire inhalation should be done gently and effortlessly. When it has been completed pause for a second or two, holding the breath. Then slowly begin breathing out. The exhalation is usually not as passive as the inhalation. You use a slight, a very slight, pressure to push the air out—although it feels as though you pressed it against the throat like a hydraulic press. The upper ribs are now contracted first, the nostrils remain inactive and the chest and shoulders motionless. At the end of the exhalation, pull in the stomach a little so as to push out all the air.

Congratulations! You have just taken your first deep breath.

Do not try to take too full a breath at once. Start by breathing to the count of four. Then hold the breath, counting to two, and start slowly exhaling, again to the count of four. Breathing in and out to an equal number of beats is called rhythmic breathing. You allow four beats to fill your lungs, two to retain the breath, and four to breathe out. The respiration should be timed in such a way that at the end of the four beats you have completed the exhalation. Don't just stop at the end of the count when there is still air to be expelled. You should adjust your breathing to the timing. Repeat, but do not take more than 5 or 6 deep breaths at one time during the first week. You shouldn't do more even if you are enjoying it.

Be careful not to overdo the breathing, especially inhalation, as this may lead to unpleasant results such as dizziness, nausea, headaches, even fainting spells due to hyperventilation caused by a sudden, excessive intake of oxygen. By practising complete breathing, you will be able to enlarge the lung capacity so that, after practice, you can inhale more air than you did before. But this increased capacity should come gradually rather than by force. By repeating such a complete breathing too often or too rapidly in succession, you may absorb too much oxygen and become dizzy. You may continue to employ all of the muscles and all portions of the lungs in breathing without expanding the lungs to their maximum extent each time you inhale.

Proper yogic breathing employs all of the muscles and all or most of the lungs. But the extent of expansion and the rate of breathing may be progressively reduced to suit the body's needs for oxygen consumption under the conditions of exercise or rest which prevail. As your cycle of breathing involves an increasingly larger lung area, your respiration may be decreased correspondingly while the amount of oxygen available for use remains the same-or even increases. Slower, deeper breathing not only stimulates the lungs into healthier action, and brings more of the body muscles into play, but it has the effect of calming the nerves. Although other factors must be taken into consideration, the slower your respiration rate the calmer you feel. You can deliberately reduce this rate for beneficial effect. However, you can maintain this only if you breathe more deeply.

A complete breath involves the following steps:

1. Inhale slowly until your lungs are filled to capacity. Some recommend that you begin with abdominal breathing, gradually move into middle breathing, and finish filling the lungs with high breathing.
2. A pause, short or long, should occur at the end of inhalation. This, too, should not be forced at first, though deliberate experiments with extending this pause play an important part in successful yogic practice.

3. Exhale, also slowly, smoothly and completely. Again, some recommend beginning exhalation with high breathing, proceeding gradually to middle breathing, and ending with abdominal breathing and use of abdominal muscles to expel all air from the lungs.
4. Another pause, short or long, should occur at the end of exhalation. This too should not be forced at first, though this pause may prove to be even more significant than the first as a stage in which to seek and find a kind of spiritual quiescence that can be most powerful in its relaxing effects.

Practise until it comes naturally to you and you can reap its calming effect.

CHAPTER 9

The Four Stages of Breathing

As we have explained before, each cycle of breathing, usually thought of as merely a single inhaling followed by a single exhaling, may be analyzed into four phases or stages, each with its distinct nature and its traditional Sanskrit name. The transitions from inhaling to exhaling and from exhaling to inhaling involve at least reversals in direction of the movements of muscles and of expansive or contractive movements of lungs, thorax and abdomen. The time necessary for such reversals can be very short, as may be observed if one deliberately pants as shortly and rapidly as he can. Yet they can be long, as one may notice if one intentionally stops breathing when one has finished inbreathing or out-breathing. The effects of these pauses specially when they become lengthened, at first deliberately and then spontaneously, seem remarkable. Thus, in our analysis of the four stages of breathing we shall pay special attention to these pauses, how to lengthen them and how to profit from them.

Inhalation

A single inhalation is termed puraka. It is a process of drawing in air; it is expected to be smooth and continuous. If a person should pause one or more times during the process of a single inhaling, the process might be spoken of as a broken puraka rather than as a series of purakas.

Pause after Inhaling—Full Pause

Kumbhaka consists of deliberate stoppage of flow of air and retention of the air in the lungs, without any movement of lungs or muscles or any part of the body and without any incipient movements. A beginner may experiment by using some force to keep such pause motionless. Quite elaborate instructions and techniques have been worked out for this purpose.

Exhalation

The third stage, exhalation, is called rechaka. Like inhalation, it too should be smooth and continuous, though often the speed of exhaling is different from that of inhaling. Normally, muscular energy is used for inhaling whereas exhaling consists merely in relaxing the tensed muscles. Such relaxing forces air from the lungs as they return to an untensed condition. However, a person can force air out with muscular effort; so when he sits or stands erect and has his abdominal muscles under constant control, muscular effort may be used for both inhaling and exhaling. Especially if one deliberately smoothes the course of his breathing and holds the cycles in regular or definitely irregular patterns, he is likely to use muscular energy at each stage, including the pauses. However, in a condition of complete relaxation, one should expect effort to be needed only for inhaling.

Pause after Exhaling—Empty Pause

The fourth stage, the pause after exhaling, is also called kumbhaka, especially when the stoppage is deliberate or prolonged. The fourth stage, the empty pause, completes the cycle which terminates as the pause ends and a new inhalation begins.

Arrested and Resting Breath

Since the two pauses have great significance in yoga, we will examine them further. Four aspects of the problem, and the significance of arresting breathing, will be explored briefly. They pertain to:

1. the length of time during a pause;
2. techniques for holding breathing;
3. suggestions concerning practice; and
4. the nature and benefits of kevala kumbhaka or "perfectly peaceful pause".

A pause may be very short, even only a fraction of a second (e.g., quick puffs) or it may be very long. As an illustration, try holding your lungs full of air and see how long you can do so. You will find that you can retain it for several seconds and even, perhaps, for minutes. If you happen to be fatigued and if your body needs constant replenishment of oxygen, you may be unable to hold your breath very long. But when you have become rested and relaxed and when your body is already well supplied with oxygen, you may hold your breath much longer. Practitioners of yoga extend the duration of a full pause by first breathing regularly for some time until the body becomes oversupplied with oxygen and then taking an extended pause without discomfort. When you try this, please remember to quit the practice when you feel the discomfort.

Advanced practitioners of yoga are said to be able to stop breathing for an hour or more without discomfort. Some of them eventually can remain almost completely motionless for days, even having themselves buried for such periods in order to demonstrate ability to survive without food, water or very much air. When buried, they do not stop breathing entirely, but their inhalations and exhalations become so long and slow and their pauses so prolonged that almost no energy is consumed and very little oxygen is needed. Even their heartbeats become so retarded that only a minimum of oxygen is needed by the heart muscles. Their cerebral activity almost ceases, so very little energy is needed to support the voracious capacity of the nervous system.

There are some significant ways of attaining relatively complete relaxation by use of these pauses between breathing. One cannot retain one's breathing for an extended duration as long as one is nervous, anxious or fatigued. So, in pursuit of extended pauses, one will have to do what is required to attain a state of rest. When you have attained full state of rest, it will result in the reduction or elimination of nervousness. It is an extremely powerful technique to incite the relaxation response.

Techniques or Aids to Prolong Pauses

There are some traditional techniques or aids available to prolong the pauses. These involve deliberate attempts to block breathing passages in such a way that air does not escape of its own accord when chest and abdominal muscles become relaxed. These aids are called bandha. Bandha is a Sanskrit word related to our English words "band," "bind," "bond" and "bound." Each of the bandha employed for prolonging breathing pauses binds air in our lungs or closes and locks the air channels so that no air can escape or enter. We will look at four important bandhas. The parts of the body mainly involved are : (a) lips and palate, (b) glottis, (c) chin and (d) diaphragm. The first two seem more important in prolonging full pauses and the last two more necessary for retaining empty pauses.

A. Bandha involving Lips and Palate

This is a technique used by swimmers. Closing our lips tightly so no air can escape through the mouth. Pressing lips against the teeth may aid in tightening them. If your nostrils are clear, simply lift your soft palate against the roof of your pharynx and close the passage into the nostrils. This may be done deliberately or you may learn to allow this to happen automatically after some training. A little air pressure from your lungs may aid in holding the palate in such a closed position.

B. Bandha involving Glottis

You can prevent air from leaving your lungs by closing your glottis. Your glottis closes automatically when you swallow. All you need to do is to stop your swallowing movements at that point where your trachea is closed. This may be difficult to do at first, since an automatic reflex pattern has been built into your autonomic nervous mechanisms. But a little effort at trying to attain voluntary control over your involuntary processes should give you mastery of this technique. Of course, you may combine both the lips and the palate closure with the glottis closure to produce a still tighter lock.

C. Jalandhara Bandha (Bandha involving Chin)

The jalandhara bandha or "chin lock" consists in pressing the chin close to the chest and dropping the head to help in maintaining immobility of muscle and air movements. This position is very useful in holding an empty pause, for the pressure of the chin against the chest pushes the

Fig. Jalandhara Bandha

base of the tongue and the larynx up into the pharynx and against the palate, thus providing aid in resisting the pressure caused by the vacuum in the lungs.

D. Uddiyana Bandha (Bandha involving Diaphragm)

A fourth bandha, uddiyana bandha, involves raising the diaphragm and keeping it immobile during an empty pause. The abdomen must be drawn in and up as far as possible. Expel all air before using this bandha. In order to attain complete control and more comfort, one may put forth some effort in one or more mock inhalations, without admitting any air, before assuming fullest relaxation possible during this pause. You may combine both chin lock and raised diaphragm techniques in retaining an empty pause. Both of these techniques can be employed in either a standing or sitting position and they are commonly employed together during sitting postures. These two bandha appear to serve as strenuous and circulation-stimulating exercises rather than muscle, and will quieting attitudes, though they do aid a person in attaining thorough mastery over his respiration cycle.

The problem of prolonging the duration of a pause should be approached with caution, patience and practice. Gradually lengthen the duration of a pause by counting. Use your fingers to count the duration of a pause. After each successive pause, add one unit of pause to the rest. If you try to attain a prolonged pause on the first attempt, you are very likely to overdo it, suffer some discomfort and feel no beneficial or restful effects. Whenever a series of increasingly extended pauses reaches the point where you feel the need to exert effort in order to hold the pause longer, stop immediately. By repeating such a series once a day for several days—or even several times a day for several days—you can observe a gradual increase in the length of the pauses which may be held with comfort. The progress you make is mainly an individual matter. Some persons can do this much more easily than others.

Kevala kumbhaka (perfectly peaceful pause) involves not only complete cessation of movement of air and muscles but also of all awareness of such movement and tendencies. The state experienced is one of complete rest. Urgency, interest, motive, will, desire, etc. all disappear momentarily along with the disappearance of specific interests and anxieties, such as those of hatred, fear, ambition, love, hunger and thirst. You will also feel detached from tendencies such as to hate specific tasks, to fear particular persons, to demand specific rights or to zealously force oneself or others to attain indicated goals. During such a peaceful pause, quiescence is experienced as perfect. For anyone writhing under the pressures of multiple anxieties, the experience of the utter peacefulness of kevala kumbhaka even for a moment, provides a very restful and blissful moment.

The experiences of kevala kumbhaka helps in retarding progressive over-anxiety that is common in our society. Suicides and suicidal tendencies, which result from the development of unbearable anxieties, may be retarded and prevented by sufficiently assiduous practice of yoga. The automatic mechanisms which spontaneously induce inhaling and exhaling, as well as heartbeats and hunger and thirst, can be modified and inhibited for short periods.

The experience of kevala kumbhaka is self-terminating and, in spite of some slight reversal of anxious tendencies, one is soon again immersed in the more usual anxieties. The experience must be repeated again and again, and even then, although it may aid in temporary reversal, it cannot be expected to overcome or counteract the much more powerful drives which nature, culture and individual ambitions have established so deeply within us. Yet, its pacifying effects should not be overlooked by anyone who has become over-ambitious and over-anxious.

The power of kevala kumbhaka and the breathing exercises are effectively tapped by combining it with the benefits of undertaking the other elements of yoga such as asanas. Although breathing can be undertaken independent of asanas and vice versa, the combination is many times more effective than doing each one of them separately. The beauty of this technique is that it is available to everyone—regardless of age, sex, occupation, religion or kind of ambition. It may be convenient to do this in the morning and evening; but you can do this at your place of work. Performing it is more relaxing and healthier than going for a cup of coffee or going to the water cooler or going for a smoke.

CHAPTER 10

Safety of Breathing Exercises

Pranayama is safe provided you follow some common sense rules. If you are suffering from a breath related problem such as asthma, emphysema, shortness of breath etc. it is only common sense to talk to your physician and get a clearance before embarking on serious breathing exercises. There are some breathing exercises that can induce dizziness or loss of consciousness. If you are prone to dizziness or loss of consciousness, avoid these exercises or assume a suitable posture to minimize problems during the exercise (such as lying down rather than standing up).

Keep in mind that the biggest problem encountered by beginning yoga students is the tendency to push beyond the limits. These exercises should be done so that they are enjoyable. Know your limits. Do not push it so that it become hard on you. If you proceed slowly and carefully, you can attain the ultimate in yoga. But it may take some time. Remember, 'slow and steady wins the race.'

Gunaji, author of 'Scientific and Efficient Breathing', recommends the following general principles:

1. Breathing exercises should never be pushed to the point of weariness or exhaustion.
2. Exercises should not be repeated too often.
3. They should not be merely mechanical.

4. There should be no hurry or haste.
5. Attention should be concentrated on the exercise while it is being performed.
6. There should always be variety and change in the exercises.
7. Exercise should always be gentle and non-violent.
8. Breathing should not be jerky or irregular, but smooth, steady and continuous.

Pranayama and other yoga breathing practices emphasize conscious breathing. As long as we pay close attention to the reaction of the body during these breathing practices, we have nothing to fear.

Problems can arise when we alter the breath and do not recognize or attend to a negative bodily reaction. If someone is labouring to breathe deeply and evenly, it will immediately become apparent; he or she will feel the need to take a quick breath in between the long, slow breaths. One important precept of Ayurvedic medicine is never to suppress the body's natural urges. Even during pranayama practice we should let ourselves take a short breath if we feel the need to do that. Pranayama should only be practised by people who can really regulate the breath. Those who suffer from chronic shortness of breath or other breathing disorders should not attempt pranayama until they are ready for it. Asanas that increase the volume of the lungs and free the muscles of the ribs, back, and diaphragm can help prepare one for pranayama. For example, a back bend and a forward bend are helpful in preparing for pranayama. An appropriate Asana practice will encourage development of pranayama. Pranayama can and should be practised in the early days of a person's discovery of yoga, and should absolutely be undertaken only with the guidance of a good teacher.

Please note that, the most important part of pranayama is the exhalation. If the quality of the exhalation is not good, the quality of the whole pranayama practice is adversely affected. When someone is not able to breathe out slowly and quietly it means that he or she is not ready for pranayama, either mentally or otherwise. Indeed, some texts give this warning: if the inhalation is rough we do not have to worry, but if the exhalation is uneven it is a sign of illness, either present or impending. Many people have the mistaken notion that the most important part is holding the breath and they do not give proper attention to the exhalation process. This is a big mistake.

Patterns of Rest between Inhalation and Exhalation

Based on the breathing patterns, specifically regarding the pattern of rest between the inhalation and exhalation, we can distinguish the following 5 types of breathing cycles:

1. No voluntary pausing occurs after either inhaling or exhaling,
2. Cessation of movement caused by deliberate effort after a full inhalation,
3. Stoppage is produced by special exertion after a thorough exhalation,
4. Voluntarily arrest inhalation at any time, and
5. Intentionally halt exhalation at any time.

You can achieve a more peaceful pause if you do not push inhalation or exhalation to extremes, especially when holding a pause at such an extreme requires some effort or strain. If you have to exert an effort to maintain the rest pauses, this will expend energy and will distract you from attaining and enjoyment of quiescence. The least strenuous conditions for pausing should be sought for maximum effectiveness.

As you become more expert in self-control, you can manage to induce pauses without effort. You will find that you can drift suddenly into a pause whenever you are willing, provided your other bodily, mental and environmental conditions permit. The degree of willingness is itself a factor both in the ease and spontaneity with which one enters a pause and in the length of time during which the pause may be enjoyed without discomfort.

Although it is possible to induce with effort or sink into a peaceful pause without any effort at any time, you will find that you can do either more conveniently and hold such a pause much longer if you prepare for it by several forced inhalings and exhalings in advance. Since the length of time during which a pause may be prolonged without discomfort depends mainly upon the supply of oxygen available in the circulatory system, any process of breathing which develops an oversupply of oxygen in the blood reduces the demands which our automatic inhalation starters make upon our respiratory muscles.

When you have prepared yourself both with easy breathing habits and with firm and comfortable posture skills, you will be ready to enjoy the fruits of peaceful pauses. The amount and effectiveness of the relaxation experienced during the pauses of even skillful practitioners will vary with the fatigue and nervous factors which must be overcome. The powerful hold that overwhelming stress has upon a person's system can be relaxed completely only by sufficiently great counter effort. No fixed rules can be given regarding how much devotion to breathing exercises is needed to vanquish the anxiety produced during any day's work struggle. Only through repeated experimentation can one develop the kind of self-knowledge and self-mastery needed to plan and execute your own programme for relaxation.

Importance of Exhalation or Breathing out in Yoga

The object of pranayama practice is to emphasize the inhalation, the exhalation, or retention of the breath. Emphasis on the inhalation is called puraka pranayama. Recaka pranayama refers to a form of pranayama in which the exhalation is lengthened while the inhalation remains free. Kumbhaka pranayama focuses on breath retention. In kumbhaka pranayama we hold the breath after inhalation, after exhalation, or after both.

As mentioned earlier, whichever technique is chosen, the most important part of pranayama is the exhalation. If the quality of the exhalation is not good, the quality of the whole pranayama practice is adversely affected. If you are not able to breathe out slowly and quietly, you are not ready for pranayama, either mentally or otherwise. "If the inhalation is rough we do not have to worry, but if the exhalation is uneven it is a sign of illness, either present or impending."

Yoga's essential aim is to eliminate impurities and reduce avidya. Through this elimination alone, positive results come about. When the blockage is cleared from a sewer pipe, the water will flow. If something in us is preventing a change from occurring, then we need to remove the obstacle before the change can take place. The exhalation is vitally important because it transports impurities from the body, making more room for prana to enter.

Often when pranayama is discussed it is the holding of the breath that is emphasized. Yet the ancient texts talk about the total breath, not simply kumbhaka, breath retention. The Yoga Sutra discusses the breath in this order of importance:

> bahya vrtti or exhalation as the most important,
> abhyantara vrtti or inhalation as secondary,
> stambha vrtti or breath retention.

All three of these are aspects of pranayama. Do not become interested only in holding the breath; many people think they can progress quickly along the yoga path by practising breath-retention techniques, but in fact problems often arise with this emphasis.

The most important tenet of pranayama is this: Only when we have emptied ourselves can we take in a new breath, and only when we can draw the breath into us can we hold it. If we cannot breathe out and in fully, how are we going to hold our breath? Breath-retention exercises must be done in such a way that they never disturb the in- and out-breaths. When we reach the stage where we have improved our ability to breathe in and out and to hold the breath, then breath-retention may become important because as it is held the breath is at rest, and with it also hopefully is the subject's mental state.

Breathing Exercises

A Breathing Exercise for Good Posture

This is an excellent exercise for the waistline or a weak back, but even more for stooped shoulders. It should be taught to all children at home and at school to counteract their tendency to slouch, for slouching, in addition to being ugly, develops a bad and unhealthy posture as it prevents the lungs from expanding as they should. It is a great exercise for beginners along with alternate nostril breathing described below:

Stand straight with feet together. Put your hands behind your back and interlock the fingers, palms upward. Now turn the palms down. This will automatically give a twisting movement to your elbows.

Inhale deeply, then bend forward, while exhaling, at the same time raising the arms until they are stretched out. Do not bend the elbows, which should remain straight throughout. Keep your head down, trying all the while to swing your arms a bit higher and higher.

Remain a moment in this position, holding your breath; then slowly return to the standing position without unlocking your fingers. Repeat the whole exercise two or three times.

Another version is done in a kneeling position. The procedure is the same, except that here you bend over until your forehead touches the floor.

Alternate Nostril Breathing

If you don't do anything else, this is a simple yoga breathing exercise that can be done virtually anywhere, anyplace. You will be glad you did.

The name alternate nostril breathing is due to the fact that we alternate between the two nostrils when we do the breathing. Yogis believe that this exercise will clean and rejuvenate your vital channels of energy, thus the name nadi sodhana (purification of nadis or channels).

With this exercise, we breathe through only one nostril at a time. The logic behind this exercise is that normal breathing does alternate from one nostril to the other at various times during the day. In a healthy person the breath will alternate between nostrils about every two hours. Because most of us are not in optimum health, this time period varies considerably between people and further reduces our vitality. According to the yogis, when the breath continues to flow in one nostril for more than two hours, as it does with most of us, it will have an adverse effect on our health. If the right nostril is involved, the result is mental and nervous disturbance. If the left nostril is involved, the result is chronic fatigue and reduced brain function. The longer the flow of breath in one nostril, the more serious the illness will be.

Benefits

1. The exercise produces optimum function to both sides of the brain: that is optimum creativity and

optimum logical verbal activity. This also creates a more balanced person, since both halves of the brain are functioning property.

2. The yogis consider this to be the best technique to calm the mind and the nervous system.

The Scientific Confirmation

Medical science has recently discovered the nasal cycle, something that was known by the yogis thousands of years ago. Scientists have recently found that we don't breathe equally with both nostrils, that one nostril is much easier to breathe through than the other at any particular time and that this alternates about every three hours. The yogis claim that the natural period is every two hours, but we must remember these studies were done on people who do not have an optimum health level.

Scientists also discovered that the nasal cycle corresponds to brain function. The electrical activity of the brain was found to be greater on the side opposite the less congested nostril. The right side of the brain controls creative activity, while the left side controls logical verbal activity. The research showed that when the left nostril was less obstructed, the right side of the brain was predominant. Test subjects were indeed found to do better on creative tests. Similarly, when the right nostril was less obstructed the left side of the brain was predominant. Test subjects did better on verbal skills.

Medical science has not quite caught up with the ancient yogis yet. The yogis went one step further. They observed that a lot of disease was due to the nasal cycle being disturbed; that is, if a person breathed for too long through one nostril. To prevent and correct this condition, they developed the alternate nostril breathing technique. This clears any blockage to air flow in the nostrils and reestablishes the natural nasal cycle. For example, the yogis have known for a long time that prolonged breathing through the left nostril only (over a period of years) will produce asthma. They also know that this so-called incurable disease can be easily eliminated by teaching the patient to breathe through the right nostril until the asthma is cured, and then to prevent it recurring by doing the alternate nostril breathing technique. The yogis also believe that diabetes is caused to a large extent by breathing mainly through the right nostril.

Technique

1. Close the right nostril with your right thumb and inhale through the left nostril. Do this to the count of four seconds.
2. Immediately close the left nostril with your right ring finger and little finger, and at the same time remove your thumb from the right nostril, and exhale through this nostril. Do this to the count of eight seconds. This completes a half round.
3. Inhale through the right nostril to the count of four seconds. Close the right nostril with your right thumb and exhale through the left nostril to the count of eight seconds. This completes one full round.

Start by doing three rounds, adding one per week until you are doing seven rounds.

Alternate nostril breathing should not be practised if you have a cold or if your nasal passages are blocked in any way. Forced breathing through the nose may lead to complications. In pranayama, it is important to follow this rule: under no circumstances should anything be forced. If you use the nostrils for breath control they must be unobstructed. If they are not, you must practise throat breathing.

Right-nostril Breathing

This refers to an exercise in which one inhales through the right nostril and exhales through the left, holding the inhaled breath as long as possible before exhaling. Although one may eventually develop an ability to do this without using the fingers to close either nostril, beginners, at least, should expect to use their fingers. You may close your nostrils in any way you choose to; but the traditional technique has become standardized as follows.

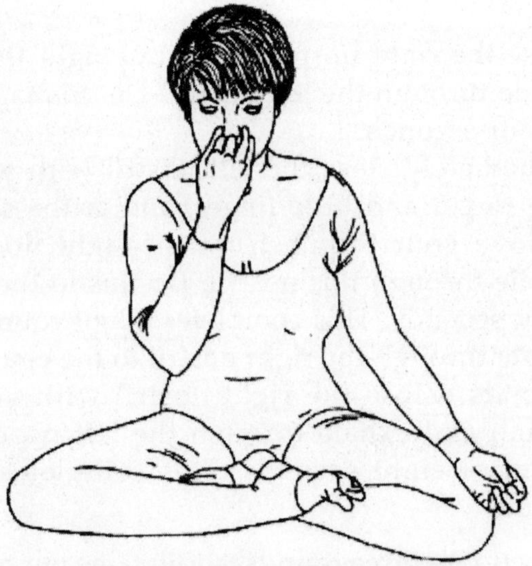

Fig. Alternate nostril breathing

After pressing the index and middle fingers of the right hand against the palm of that hand, use the thumb to close the right nostril and the ring and little fingers to close the left nostril. Left-handed persons may reverse this procedure. When both nostrils are open, the fingers rest on the bridge of the nose.

Properly performed, both inhalation and exhalation should be complete, and the process repeated ten to twenty times without pausing between cycles (with a prolonged full pause but no empty pause), and with continuous voluntary control over one's muscles to assure smooth, soundless breathing at all times. One should employ both the "chin lock" (jalandhara bandha) and diaphragm raising (uddiyana bandha); he may use the lips and palate and glottis closures also if he chooses. Although one should never hold his breath to produce undue strain, still one is expected to feel, sooner or later, a pressure all over one's body, from head to toes, or from the roots of his hair to the tips of his toenails, with perspiration oozing from one's pores. Climatic conditions and amount of surplus water in one's body may have some bearing upon the result. But repetition of this exercise may enable one to continue it, after much practice, to as many as eighty repetitions in a series without discomfort.

The "Loud Breathing"

This consists in drawing air in through both nostrils with the glottis held partially closed. Ujjayi translates as "what clears the throat and masters the chest area." This partial closure of the glottis produces a sound like that heard in sobbing, except that it is continuous and unbroken. The sound should have a low but uniform pitch and be pleasant to hear. Friction of air in the nose should be avoided; consequently, no nasal sounds will be heard. A prolonged full pause should begin, without any jerking, as soon as inhalation has been completed. Closure of glottis, use of chin lock and closure of both nostrils are standard. Prolong the pause as long as possible; but it should be terminated and exhalation commenced smoothly and slowly. When properly performed, exhalation proceeds slowly and steadily through the left nostril with the glottis partially closed as in inhalation. One may begin to exhale with release of air pressure by lifting the finger from his left nostril, loosening his chin lock and then partially opening his glottis. Exhalation should be complete.

Ujjayi breathing has many variations. For example, we can breathe in through the throat, then completely close one nostril and breathe out through the other nostril, which is only partly closed. This technique is called an anuloma ujjayi. In a pranayama technique called viloma ujjayi, we breathe in through the nostril and breathe out through the throat. This technique is used to lengthen the inhalation. In ujjayi pranayama it is important to follow this rule: when we regulate the breath through the nostril, we never breathe through the throat at the same time.

Although the total length of time required for a single cycle of breathing will vary with different persons, certain ratios of the periods needed for inhaling, pausing and exhaling are recommended. The period occupied by exhaling should be about twice as long as that occupied by inhaling. Practise inhaling and exhaling without a full pause. Then, when you feel ready, hold your breathing for a pause which is comfortable. With continued practice, this pause can be extended to a duration which is double that of the inhalation or equal to that of the exhalation. Advanced practitioners of yoga hold their pauses to four times the duration of inhalation and double the duration of exhalation.

Rhythmic Breathing

Yoga enthusiasts say that by practising rhythmic breathing you become attuned to the rhythm of the Universe. Rhythmic breathing helps you establish a direct contact with the whole world. You come to experience a sense of oneness with the universe. The result is that the feeling of separateness disappears and with it fear, loneliness, frustration, doubt, despair and other miseries. Rhythmic breathing is a great exercise for relaxation.

Benefits

- Increased oxygen supply (even more than deep breathing)
- Re-establishes the body's own natural rhythm
- Helps you to acquire self-confidence, optimism, a calm mind or any other desired quality.

Rhythmic breathing, as well as correct concentration and meditation, can bring about a great change in both your physical and mental state and serve as a step toward spiritual unfolding.

Everything in the universe is in vibration, from the atom to the planets themselves. In all vibration there exists a certain rhythm, so rhythm pervades the universe. The movement of the planets around the sun, the ebb and flow of the tide, all follow rhythmic laws.

Our bodies are also subject to rhythmic laws called biorhythms. Sleep and waking periods also have a rhythm. Sleep is governed by the steep cycle. The waking period has precise cycles of varying metabolic rates which differ between individuals. Some people are wide awake early in the morning, while others reach their peak efficiency in the afternoon or evening.

The yogis say that the deep rhythmic breathing exercise will allow the body to re-establish its own natural rhythm and attune us more to the cosmic rhythm. This will protect us from any negative external influences.

The deep rhythmic breathing exercise, by falling in with the rhythm of the body, also allows the body to absorb a lot, more oxygen than just normal deep breathing.

Technique

Rhythmic breathing is done in the same way as deep breathing, but it is timed to the rhythm of your heartbeat. Inhalation and exhalation should be done to the same number of beats, as this establishes an even rhythm.

Fig. Postures for rhythmic breathing

First assume the correct posture. If you cannot comfortably remain in the Lotus Pose, get into an easy cross-legged position or even sit on a chair. Remember to open your belt, unhook your bra, loosen your girdle or tie if you happen to be wearing any of these items. Keep the spine straight, with hands on knees, and start by taking a few deep breaths, and then stop.

Now put the second, third and fourth fingers of your right hand on the left wrist to find the pulse. Carefully listen to the pulse beat, and after a short while start counting 1-2-3-4 several times, to the rhythm of the beats.

Continue mentally counting 1-2-3-4, 1-2-3-4 until you fall into this rhythm and can follow it without holding your pulse. Then put your hands on your knees and take a deep breath while counting 1-2-3-4; hold the breath while counting 1-2; exhale while again counting 1-2-3-4.

1. Sit up straight, either on a chair or cross-legged on the floor. Let your hands just rest on your lap.
2. Inhale slowly and deeply for eight seconds. Push your stomach forwards, to a count of four seconds, and then push your ribs sideways for a count of two seconds, and then finally lift your chest and

collar bone upwards for a count of two seconds. This makes a total of eight seconds.

3. Don't breathe out immediately; instead hold the breath (called retention) for four seconds.
4. Exhale slowly for eight seconds. For the first six seconds just allow the collar bone, chest and ribs to relax, so the breath goes out automatically. For the last two seconds, push the stomach in gently, to expel all the air from the lungs.
5. Keep the stomach in this position for four seconds before you take the next breath.

Do the above exercise three times the first week, and add one more round each week, until you are doing seven breaths. It's best to build up the number of breaths gradually, because if you are not used to doing yoga breathing and you overdo it, you will purify your system too quickly. This will cause your body to release toxins from your tissues into the blood circulation too quickly, resulting in unpleasant symptoms such as headaches, skin rashes and fatigue.

The yogi rule for rhythmic breathing is that the units of inhalation and exhalation should be the same, while the units for retention and between breaths should be half that of inhalation and exhalation; that is, a ratio of 2:1:2:1.

Sometimes beginners find that inhaling for eight seconds is too difficult. If this is the case, inhale for six seconds, hold the breath for three seconds, exhale for six seconds, and pause for three seconds before taking the next breath. In a few weeks you will easily be able to do 8:4:8:4.

Rhythmic Breathing with Visualization

The rhythmic breathing exercise is made much more potent if you use visualization while doing the breathing.

Visualization works on the principle that whatever you concentrate on, an extra supply of oxygen and prana (life force) will be directed to that area. The secret of successful yoga is combining the exercise with visualizing the specific area the exercise affects.

The technique is simple. When you breathe in, visualize the prana accumulating in the solar plexus area, just above the navel, behind the stomach. The solar plexus is where the body stores its energy. When you retain the breath and breathe out, visualize the prana going to the brain. Just concentrate on the brain area.

This visualization technique achieves two things. Firstly, it produces a reserve of energy in the solar plexus, thereby increasing your general energy level. Second, since some of the stored energy is directed to the brain, brain function and vitality are increased.

Frequency

The rhythmic breathing exercise can be done on the morning and in the evening. Do not overdo this in the beginning. Start with three or four rounds, adding one round per week until you finally reach the desired number, perhaps sixty or more.

This exercise can also be done with different asanas, if lotus pose is too difficult for you.

Walking Breathing Exercise

Walking Breathing exercise is done in exactly the same way as Rhythmic Breathing except that you do it while walking. Use each step as a count, as the pulse beat used in Rhythmic Breathing.

Stand erect, exhale first, then start walking, right foot first. Take four steps while inhaling, hold the breath in for two steps, exhale for four steps, and hold the breath out for two steps. Without stopping, continue the routine: inhale on four steps, hold the breath in for two steps, and so forth. Do not interrupt the walking—keep it rhythmical. The breathing should be done in one continuous flow: do not inhale in four short breaths, a mistake which many beginners tend to make. Inhale one deep breath to the count of four, hold it to the count of two, exhale it to the count of four, and again hold the emptiness to the count of two. This completes one round. Make five such rounds a day the first week—no more—adding one round per week.

If you feel that four steps are too long for you, count three steps and hold one. If, on the contrary, four are not enough and you feel you want to continue the inhalation, take six steps or even eight, and hold the breath on a count of three or four steps respectively. In either case, you should take an even number of steps while breathing in and out, as the retention is done in half the time taken for inhalation or exhalation.

You can do the Walking Breathing exercise at any other time while you are exercising, walking, especially when the air is clean—in a park, a forest, or at the seashore. You can do it while walking to your car or bus, descending a staircase, on your way to pick up your mail from the letter box, during a coffee break in your office, in fact, whenever you think of it. Simply interrupt your usual walking tempo, stop to inhale and exhale deeply. Then start rhythmic breathing to the count of slow and even steps.

Conclude your lesson by doing the relaxation and meditation.

Teeth Hissing

Sitkari pertains to the sound made by drawing air in through the front teeth—either tightly closed or slightly opened—with the tongue tip regulating the air pressure and sound. This technique pertains only to inhaling, except that exhaling normally takes place through both nostrils, after a usual full pause. The sides of the tongue are pressed against the teeth lining the sides of the mouth, if they are closed tightly, or expanding between the upper and lower sets, if the jaw is opened slightly. The sound, a kind of reversed hissing, like that made when one suddenly touches ice or a hot object or feels a draft of hot or frigid air, should be regulated so as to be smooth and to sound pleasant. The experience has been described as "sipping air." This technique usually cools the mouth and may have both a cooling and a relaxing effect upon the whole body. Lips should close at the end of inhalation, preparatory to holding the full pause with chin lock. Closure of the lips ends the hissing sound, si, with a "sip".

Tongue Hissing

Sitali refers to the sound caused when air is drawn in through the protruding tongue folded into a tube. During inhalation, curl up both edges of the tongue so that it forms a kind of tube. Breathe in through this tube. During inhalation the air passes over the moist tongue, cooling down and refreshing the throat. In order to be sure that the tongue remains moist, roll it back as far as possible against the palate. Do this during the entire exhalation so that the next breath is just as refreshing as the first. The resulting tongue position may appear more like the lower portion of a bird's beak than a tube, but variable opening or closing of the tube-like passage in the folded tongue, in cooperation with faster or slower inhalation, makes possible variations in loudness and softness and smoothness of the reversed hissing sound. Again, a cooling effect may be noted and, indeed, sought through this and the foregoing technique whenever needed. The tongue is drawn back into the mouth and the lips are closed at the end of inhalation. We can breathe out either through the throat or alternately through the nostrils.

The Cleansing Breath

The Cleansing Breath, as its name indicates, cleans and ventilates the lungs; it also tones up the entire system. You should do the Cleansing Breath at the end of other yoga exercises or just before the final relaxation exercises.

To do the Cleansing Breath, stand straight with feet close together and arms hanging loosely at the sides. Take a deep breath, hold it for a little while, then purse your lips as if you were going to whistle. Now start exhaling forcefully, little by little, but do not blow the air out as if you were blowing out a candle, and do not puff out the cheeks. They should be hollowed.

These successive and forceful exhalations will feel almost like slight coughs which expel the air until the lungs are completely empty. The effort of the exhalation should be felt in the chest and in the back.

Rest for a little while, then repeat. After a week you may repeat this routine several times a day.

Bellows

Bhastrika consists primarily in forced rapid deep breathing which serves as a basis for many varieties of exercises, all of which may be described by the same name. Although air is forced both in and out, emphasis is placed upon expulsion or explosion of air. A series of such explosions, each following the other in quick succession without pause, either full or empty, may be called "a round". Beginners should limit a round to about five explosions, though the number may be increased to ten, or to any number needed to obtain the desired effect. The desired effects range from increased ventilation, increased blood circulation, increased clearing of nasal passages and increased thinking capacity to overwhelming pacification of all mental disturbances. Please be warned against generating such powerful explosions that the lung tissues will be injured and against extending a series so long as to become dizzy. Comfort, not reckless excess, should guide your motives and manner in doing this exercise.

Although you can breathe through your mouth or both mouth and nose, traditionally breathing is limited to either both nostrils or one nostril. The breath-stroke in the rapid succession of breaths may or may not be very deep, but it is customary to finish or follow a round by the deepest possible inhalation and exhalation. A series of normal breaths should occur before undertaking a second round. A deepest possible inhalation and exhalation may, and perhaps should, introduce each round. Some nasal hissing can be expected; avoid unpleasant sound and fluttering of nasal skin surfaces. Although you can stand if you wish, proper performance of this technique is done in a seated position allowing maximum relaxation of abdominal muscles and easy diaphragmatic breathing. Variations include using a full pause after each round, partial glottis closures and alternation of nostrils.

You should exercise caution against the temptation to go to excess in initial bellows experiments. If you have a tendency to push the limit, lie down when doing this exercise if there is any danger of losing consciousness and falling to the floor. Forced breathing produces relaxation and revitalization. Excess may induce dizziness, drowsiness and diminution of consciousness. No harm can come from hyperventilation so long as you are in bed. If you happen to lose consciousness your breathing pattern tends to rectify itself and return to normalcy. Excessive ventilation results in light-heartedness, giddiness or a feeling of floating in the air.

Cleansing Breath

Kapalabhati is a breathing technique used specifically for cleansing. If we have a lot of mucus in the air passages or feel tension and blockages in the chest it is often helpful to breathe quickly. In this practice we deliberately breathe faster, and at the same time use only abdominal (that is, diaphragmatic) breathing, not chest breathing. In kapalabhati the breath is short, rapid, and strong. We use the lungs as a pump, creating so much pressure as they expel the air that all the rubbish is cleared from the air passages, from the lungs up through the nostrils. Kapala means "skull," and bhati means "that which brings lightness." Kapalabhati is a good thing to do when we feel heavy or foggy in the head. If we have problems with the sinuses or feel numb around the eyes, kapalabhati can help to clear this area as well.

The kapalabhati and bhastrika breathing techniques share the same general principle, namely that we clear the nasal passages with the force of the breath. As mentioned under bhastrika, we must be very careful with these techniques because there is a danger of creating tension in the breath. We may also become dizzy when we breathe rapidly; for this reason we always conclude the practice of kapalabhati with some slow breaths. It is important not to breathe rapidly too many times, but after a few rapid breaths take several slow ones in which we emphasize the long exhalation.

Nasal Snoring

Bhramari differs from the usual mouth snoring in that the lips are closed and vibrations of the soft palate are caused entirely by nasal airflow. Practise mouth snoring first in order to develop some voluntary control over the palate vibration process. Nasal snoring is more difficult. Approach control attempts gradually. The soft palate must be lifted toward the top of the pharynx sufficiently to produced flutter which may be very hard to control. The sound produced is commonly described as being like the buzzing of a bee. Although, in bhramari, one breathes both in and out through both nostrils and produces a snoring, buzzing or humming sound in both directions, expect somewhat different sounds from inhaling, which has a higher pitch, than from exhaling, which has a lower pitch. Bhramari is customarily described as involving rapid inhalation producing a high humming sound like that of a male bee and slow exhalation producing a low humming sound like that of a female bee.

Swooning

This exercise is recommended only for those already well advanced in the use of other breathing techniques. Its maximum benefit comes from repeated practice under controlled conditions wherein the practitioner knows what to expect. It involves a prolonged full pause held with a chin lock, until you experience the approach of fainting. Beginners may, indeed, faint. But experts remain seated upright, normally in the Lotus Posture, and attain a restful, pleasant suspension of consciousness. One breathes through both nostrils and may require several rounds and full pauses to attain his goal. If the approaching fainting appears to be leading to a collapse of posture, one may resist it until are regains physical self-control. When successful, one enjoys a prolonged, relaxed, euphorious, semiconscious swoon.

Floating

Plavini is not so much a breathing technique for getting air into the lungs as an air-swallowing technique for getting air into the belly. By both swallowing air until the stomach is bloated, when it sounds something like a drum if tapped, and keeping the lungs almost fully inflated, one can float in water for an indefinite time if otherwise undisturbed. By retaining a prolonged full pause and exhaling and inhaling very slowly, one is able, with the aid of an air-filled stomach, to remain afloat with comfort. This method may be combined with mineral baths, hot baths or other bathing techniques designed for relaxing, and with various postures, such as the Fish Posture, which can be performed easily in water. However, plavini, like other breathing exercises, may also be practised in a normal seated position. Whether the relaxation which comes from this exercise seems worthwhile is something you should judge for yourself. Those suffering from stomach gas pains should avoid this method, unless they also master ways for expelling air through the esophagus (by belching or eructation) or anus (after learning from posture exercises which most effectively achieve this end) as needed.

Taoist Relaxation Breathing

Although, in a sense, all yogic breathing exercises may be employed for relaxing, as well as revitalization and increased self-control, Taoist Yoga is especially good for relaxation and to remove anxiety. It gives prompt, quick relief. However, the effects can be quite temporary. Therefore, special efforts must be made to prolong and deepen these results by subtle, attentive, repeated, devotion.

The Taoist relaxation method is very simple: "Listen to your breathing." Nothing more is needed, except persistence and patience in such listening. If you do not persist, your attention will stray back into anxieties. Be patient; impatience merely adds to anxieties. Patience is an attitude which undercuts the roots of anxiety. The healing, revitalizing and relaxing effect of attending to one's breathing may be observed by giving it a trial. Breathing involves inhalation (yang) followed by exhalation (yin), that these succeed each other in a natural, rhythmic, continuing and reliable order. When you devote yourself to Nature's Way (Tao) all goes well. When you attend to your breathing, you tend to take deeper breath and you also gradually prolong it, and, in the process quiets your fluttering mental activities as the mind harmonizes itself with the slower, and slowing, rhythm of the breathing. By listening, you must focus your attention on the sound; thereby withdrawing it from whatever has been disturbing, exciting and fatiguing the mind. Of all the ways for seeking relaxation, none can be more harmless than this. No outside help, no drugs, no devices, no special skills, no muscular effort, no training period, no involved instructions are needed for successful use. It can be used anytime, anywhere, by anyone who has a few moments to spare.

Unfortunately, most of those who begin to try out this Taoist technique will give up too soon and drift into the conclusion that their experiment was a failure. How long does one have to listen to the breathing? Why not as long as one feels fatigue? If the method is to be effective, you must persist until you feel the effects. Keep listening until "you finally do not hear it." Listen to your breathing with undivided attention until you do not hear it any more. When you have persisted with patience until this happens, your anxieties should be considerably lessened. There is nothing, of course, to prevent you from arousing them again, when you turn your attention back to their initiating objects, persons or activities. But one who has pacified himself with such a relaxing pause should have a bit more reserve energy to cope with his task. The traditional Taoist seeks self-containment; this technique requires nothing more than opportunity and will to escape from the demands made upon self by externals, and the ability and will to listen to one's own self-made sounds until they can be heard no more. Whether one then sleeps or finds his attention occupied by other things, the surrendering of his attentiveness to the sounds of his breathing has occurred without further mental disturbance.

Chang said merely, "Listen to your breathing. Till finally you do not hear." This intuitively clear, common-sense advice can only be distorted by complex elaboration. Chang demonstrated with a slow breathing cycle and with a manner in which an enveloping quiescence was intuitively sensed. One who cannot grasp what is simple can hardly expect to comprehend it when it has been made complex.

CHAPTER 11

Corrective Breathing Therapy

Functions of Breathing

Respiration is a complex psycho-biological function that serves a number of purposes: (1) air passage: ventilation, sound production and smelling; (2) rhythmic volume changes: a central 'pumping action', involved in internal movement of air, fluids, organs, spinal column and in external body movement and balance; (3) sensory awareness of the body: internal tension state and external place of the body in space.

Disturbance of any of these functions can be caused by somatic or mental factors. It can also be caused by a disturbance in respiration itself. Often, there is a combination of a somatic or psychological cause and a functional disturbance of respiration itself. The term 'Dysfunctional Breathing' (DB) refers to disturbance in any of the above respiratory functions, as far as there is no adequate physical or mental cause for it. Such dysfunctional breathing is involved in for instance lung diseases, postural problems, anxiety and hyperventilation complaints. It can also be involved in the origin and maintenance of voice disorders (stuttering, functional dysphonia).

The degree to which DB is involved in the origin or maintenance of complaints and disorders can be assessed by the attempt to restore functional breathing. Thus, restoration of functional breathing by way of breathing therapy is important in both the differential diagnostic effort to assess the cause of the trouble, and in the actual treatment. The diagnosis of DB can be made with certainty only in retrospect: DB was present to the degree that restoration of functional breathing was possible and that this coincided with amelioration of the problem.

Characteristics of Functional Breathing

Under optimal physical and mental conditions functional breathing has the following characteristics:

- Air passage is soundless.
- Transitions between inhaling and exhaling are smooth, non-abrupt.
- Rhythmic volume changes occur all over the trunk.
- These volume changes are perceptible to the subject.
- There is a co-ordination of ribcage and abdomen with spinal column motion.
- It is responsive to, for instance, movement, touch and mental imagery.

The functionality of breathing should be assessed and corrected under optimal, resting conditions, without active voice production. The role of DB can be established within a few (3-4) individual sessions. Assessment consists of procedures that elicit changes in the direction of more functional breathing. They are specifically developed verbal instructions and manual techniques. There are four possible outcomes:

1. When respiration responds to them and there is also a response in the complaints, there is an indication for continuation of breathing therapy.
2. When respiration responds, but there is no change in the complaints at all, there is a reason to doubt the causative role of DB in the origin or maintenance of the trouble.
3. When respiration does not respond and there is little

or no change in the direction of more functional breathing, there are to all probability specific factors that limit the possibility for change. These may be somatic or mental causes or the dysfunctional pattern may be thoroughly ingrained and resistant to quick change.

4. When respiration does not respond, but the complaints do improve, the reason for the improvement is not related to the specific influence of the treatment, but due to aspecific influences (placebo-effect) or due to simultaneous changes in the somatic or psychic causes.

Breathing Therapy

The procedures of breathing therapy focus mostly on the functions of rhythmic volume change and sensory awareness. The normal respiration pattern can be classified into two forms, dependent upon the co-ordination with the spinal column.

When the spinal column is straight and the body is lying supine or sitting or standing upright, the normal respiration movement form is one of extension of the spinal column during inhalation and flexion during exhalation. The lumbar lordosis increases slightly during inhalation, thus lifting the thorax and increasing the distance between symphysis and chestbone (xyfoid process). The upper spine flattens somewhat during inhalation, but the cervical lordosis increases somewhat during exhalation. Thus, the thorax changes shape and increases in volume, but also rolls a little upwards during inhalation and downward during exhalation.

The presence of this normal pattern can be assessed for instance in the supine position as follows. The clinician presses the spinal column softly with one hand under the lumbar spine and the other under the upper thoracic spine. After some time, the resistance to pressure is lower in the lumbar spine during inhalation than during exhalation and the pressure increases inhalation a little. The resistance to pressure is lower in the upper thoracic spine during exhalation than during inhalation, and the pressure stimulates exhalation. The degree of sensory awareness can be assessed by asking the subject about the perception of the effect of the pressure on respiration. When the body is relaxed and the mental state is relatively quiet, the spinal column allows the effect of pressure to influence respiration and this is perceived passively. There is no urge to modify respiration consciously, the changes are simply perceived.

This normal pattern tends to become easily exaggerated. It is the most common dysfunctional breathing pattern: the lumbar lordosis loses flexibility and becomes stiff in the extended state. This is shown by difficulty in obtaining the second respiration form.

The second respiration form is the opposite of the first pattern. It occurs naturally when the spinal column is flexed, as for instance when sitting in a slump posture or lying curled up on the side. During inhalation the lumbar lordosis flattens and flexes even more. The upper thoracic area flexes as well. This allows for the lower ribs to spread and elevate maximally. The thorax does not roll upwards during inhalation and the body does not extend. The body widens sideways.

The presence of this pattern can be assessed for instance in the sitting position, by way of the hands of the clinician on either side of the spinal lumbar column, with the thumbs medially and the fingers spread out laterally. When the ribs elevate and spread laterally during inhalation, and the head and upper body do not rise, the pattern of sideways expansion is present. It can be strengthened by adding medial pressure on the ribs during exhalation. When this leads to gradually increased lateral spreading with inhalation, the pattern is clearly present. A relaxed mental and physical state favours this respiratory pattern. The body weight is clearly perceived, the back is not straightened with effort, respiration is allowed its natural course in this position. The effect of adding pressure with exhalation on the ribs, or of stimulating respiration by audible exhaling through slightly pursed lips, is simply perceived and can be described by the subject.

Both of these patterns can be elicited by way of changing posture. For instance, in the sitting position, when the body is moved easily forward and backward, while the head remains pointed at more or less the same angle. The forward movement tends to elicit inhalation with extension of the spine, the backward movement tends to elicit inhalation with lateral spreading. A fully flexible respiration can switch easily between both patterns. This is assessed by having the person remain in one position and continue to breathe in and out. Then, by changing the posture and again breathe in and out a number of times, the opposite pattern is tested.

The existence of the two patterns implies that so-called 'abdominal breathing' is not the best or most natural or relaxed or efficient breathing pattern. Flexibility of the spine, together with volume changes in both abdomen and chest is more important than movement in one compartment of the body. In the first pattern, extension of the spine facilitates abdominal expansion, while at the same time the chest is elevated. There is adequate costo-abdominal co-ordination and there is no point to try and limit the expansion of the chest and elevation of the chestbone. In so-called 'upper-thoracic breathing', the speed of inhalation is increased and the chestbone raises while at the same time abdominal expansion lessens. Thus, the problem is not the chest movement, but the lack of adequate co-ordination. In the second pattern, sideways expansion limits abdominal movement forward somewhat. When the abdomen relaxes however, the whole of the lower body widens with inhalation, including the pelvic area. Respiratory movement in the pelvic area facilitates awareness of this area, which in turns promotes a relaxed sitting posture. The posture shows a relatively round back, but does not become too slumped, because of contracting the lower ribs and abdomen with exhalation.

Voice Production

Voice production, particularly singing, is a form of activity that requires respiratory effort. It goes beyond the area of breathing therapy to coach subjects in this activity. However, the effects of breathing therapy are often noticeable. First, it facilitates the return to the normal, relaxed respiration pattern after the activity. The subjects recovers more quickly and more fully after a period of intense use of the voice. Second, voice production itself becomes easier. Often, after some of the procedures that stimulate both patterns, the voice becomes more clear and strong.

The concept and practice of so-called 'breath support' becomes more clear with the understanding of the two patterns of breathing. In the standing position, the body tends to extend with inhalation. However, with 'breath support' inhalation retains also strong sideways expansion in the lumbar area. This is stimulated by retaining full awareness of the weight and pressure of the body to the floor and of the area of the back. Thus, the body is filled up maximally with relatively little effort. The head does not come forward or look up, but flattening of the cervico-thoracic junction brings the chin slightly backwards and facilitates raising the chestbone. 'Breath support' in the upper area of the body means to maintain this inhalation position during exhalation. The normal pattern of the thorax rolling down with exhalation is stopped and replaced by remaining in the extended state. 'Breath support' in the lower area of the body means to retain the sideways and forward expansion of inhalation in the abdomen and pelvis during exhalation. Exclusive focus on the lower area of support diminishes the support in the upper area. Thus, the focus of support can shift up and down the body.

Chapter 12

Meditative Breathing

Most forms of meditation regulate breathing during the period of meditation. Some achieve this by just being aware of the breath as it touches the nostrils on the way into the nose and out, during the period of meditation. Others achieve it by repeating one-word mantra silently for twenty minutes, twice a day, which helps to slow and deepen one's breathing during meditation. Thus part of the benefits of meditation discussed below are due to its regulated breathing component.

Generic Meditation Method

This method is from the book, *Timeless Healing* (1996), by Herbert Benson with Marg Stark, published by Simon and Schuster. Variations on this technique have been found to have many positive mental and physical effects on people who use it once or twice a day for 10 to 20 minutes.

1. Pick a focus word or short phrase that's firmly rooted inyour belief system.
2. Sit quietly in a comfortable position.
3. Close your eyes.
4. Relax your muscles.
5. Breath slowly and naturally, and as you do, repeat your focus word, pharase, or prayer silently to yourself as you exhale.

6. Assume a passive attitude. Don't worry about how well you're doing. When other thoughts come to mind, simply say to yourself, "Oh, well," and gently return to the repetition.
7. Continue for ten to twenty minutes.
8. Do not stand immediately. Continue sitting quietly for a minute or so, allowing other thoughts to return. Then open your eyes and sit for another minutes before rising.
9. Practise this technique once or twice daily.

How Meditation Works

Studies have shown that meditation can bring about a healthy state of relaxation by causing a generalized reduction in multiple physiological and biochemical markers, such as decreased heart rate, decreased respiration rate, decreased plasma cortisol (a major stress hormone), decreased pulse rate, and increased EEG (electroencephalogram) alpha, a brain wave associated with relaxation. Research conducted by R. Keith Wallace at U.C.L.A. on Transcendental Meditation, revealed that during meditation, the body gains a state of profound rest. At the same time, the brain and mind become more alert, indicating a state of restful alertness. Studies show that after TM, reactions are faster, creativity greater, and comprehension broader.

A laboratory study of practitioners of Maharishi Mahesh Yogi's transcendental meditation (TM), carried out by Benson and Wallace at Harvard Medical School towards the end of the 1960s, provided the first detailed knowledge of the many physiological changes that go with meditation.

Some of the meditators, whose ages ranged from seventeen to forty-one, had been meditating only a few weeks, others for several years. All recorded changes associated with deep relaxation.

The fall in metabolic rate was the most striking discovery. This was indicated by a dramatic drop in oxygen consumption within a few minutes of starting meditation. Consumption fell by up to twenty per cent below the normal level; below that experienced even in deep sleep. Meditators took on average two breaths less and one litre less air per minute. The meditators' heart rate was several beats less per minute.

During meditation, blood pressure stayed at 'low levels', but fell markedly in persons starting meditation with abnormally high levels.

The meditators' skin resistance to an electrical current was measured. A fall in skin resistance is characteristic of anxiety and tension states; a rise indicates increased muscle relaxation. The finding was that though meditation is primarily a mental technique, it soon brings significantly improved muscle relaxation.

Meditation reduces activity in the nervous system. The parasympathetic branch of the autonomic or involuntary nervous system predominates. This is the branch responsible for calming us.

During anxiety and tension states there is a rise in the level of lactate in the blood.

Lactate is a substance produced by metabolism in the skeletal muscles. During meditation blood lactate levels decreased at a rate four times faster than the rate of decrease in non-meditators resting lying on their backs or in the meditators themselves in pre-meditation resting.

The likely reason for the dramatic reduction in lactate production by meditators was indicated when further studies of meditators showed an increased blood flow during. Benson and Wallace found that there was a thirty-two per cent increase in forearm blood flow. Lactate production in the body is mainly in skeletal muscle tissue; during meditation the faster circulation brings a faster delivery of oxygen to the muscles and less lactate is produced.

The two investigators summed up the state produced by their meditating subjects as wakeful and hypometabolic. The physiological changes were different in many ways from those found in sleeping people or those in hypnotic trance states. Meditation, they said, produces 'a complex of responses that marks a highly relaxed state'. Moreover, the pattern of changes they observed in meditators suggested an integrated response, mediated by the central nervous system.

"Through meditation we can learn to access the relaxation response (the physiological response elicited by meditation) and to be aware of the mind and the way our attitudes produce stress," says Dr. Joan Borysenko, author of 'Minding the Body, Mending the Mind". "In addition, by quieting the mind, meditation can also put one in touch with the inner physician, allowing the body's own inner wisdom to be heard."

Taoists believe that the mind of emotions is governed by the Fire energy of the heart. When your emotions are not controlled, the fire energy of the heart flares upwards, wastefully burning up energy and clouding the mind. The mind of intent, or willpower, is controlled by the Water energy of the kidneys. When unattended, the water energy flows down and out through the sexual organs, depleting essence and energy and weakening the spirit. Taoists believe that when you are 'sitting still, doing nothing', as in meditation, the flow of Fire and Water are reversed: Water energy from the kidneys and sacrum is drawn up to the head via the Central and Governing channels, while emotional Fire energy from the heart is drawn down into the Lower Elixir Field in the abdomen, where it is refined and transformed and enters general circulation through the energy channels. On the spiritual/mental level, this internal energy alchemy enables the mind of intent (Water) to exert a calming, cooling, controlling influence over the mind of emotion (Fire).

CHAPTER 13

Research from Harvard's Mind/Body Clinic

The following results were found in research at Harvard's *Mind/Body Clinic* with people who were taught a simple meditation technique of the type described in Chapter 12, and in some of the research below this was combined with other self-care strategies such as nutrition, exercise, and/or stress management.

Patients with hypertension experienced significant decreases in blood pressure and needed fewer or no medications over a three-year measurement period (Stuart et al., 1987).

- Patients with chronic pain experienced less severity of pain, more activity, less anxiety, less depression, less anger, and they visited the managed care facility where they received care 36 per cent less often in the two years after completing the program than they did prior to treatment (Caudill, Schnable, Zuttermeister, Benson, & Friedman, 1991).
- Seventy-five per cent of patients with sleep-onset insomnia (meaning that they couldn't fall asleep easily) were cured and became normal sleepers. Sleeping also improved for the other 25 per cent, and most patients took significantly fewer sleep medications (Jacobs, Benson, & Friedman, 1993).

- Thirty-six percent of women with unexplained infertility became pregnant within six months of completing the programme (Domar, Zuttermeister, Seibel, & Benson, 1992).
- Patients with complaints described by the admitting personnel as psychosomatic and who were frequent users of a health maintenance organization reduced their number of visits by 50 per cent (Hellman, Budd, Borysenko, McClelland, & Benson, 1990).
- Women suffering from symptoms of premenstrual syndrome (PMS) experienced a 57 percent decrease in severity. The more severe the PMS, the more effective the relief with the relaxation response (Goodale, Domar, & Benson, 1990).
- Patients with cardiac arhythmias experienced fewer of them (Benson, Alexander, & Fieldman, 1975).
- Patients who suffered from anxiety or mild or moderate depression were less anxious, depressed, angry, and hostile (Benson et al., 1978).
- Patients undergoing painful X-ray procedures experienced less anxiety and pain and needed one-third the amount of pain and anxiety medications usually required (Mandle et al., 1990).
- Patients who had open-heart surgery had fewer postoperative arrhythmias and less anxiety following surgery (Lesserman, Stuart, Mamish, & Benson, 1989).
- Migraine and cluster headache sufferers found they had fewer and less severe headaches (Benson, Klemchuk, & Graham, 1974).
- High school sophomores increased their self-esteem (Benson et al., 1994).
- Working people experienced reduced symptoms of depression, anxiety, and hostility (Carrington et al., 1980).

- Working people had fewer medical symptoms, fewer illness days, improved performance, and lower blood pressure (Peters, Benson, & Peters, 1977).

Healing Power of Meditation

Research has shown that meditation can contribute to an individual's psychological and physiological well-being. This is accomplished as meditation brings the brainwave pattern into an alpha state, which is a level of consciousness that promotes the healing state.

Patricia Norris, Ph.D., Director of the Biofeedback and Psychophysiology Clinic at the Menninger Foundation, reports: "In our practice at Menninger we use meditative techniques to enhance immune functioning in cancer, AIDS, and autoimmune patients. We also use meditation in conjunction with neuro-feedback to normalize brain rhythms and chemistry in alcohol and drug addiction, as well as other addictive conditions. Almost all of our patients use meditative techniques in learning self-regulation for disorders such as anxiety and hypertension, and for stress management. We consider meditation a recommended practice for anyone seeking high-level wellness."

In addition to the growing body of research literature on meditation, physicians, psychotherapists, and other professionals are increasingly adding meditative techniques to their practice. Over six thousand physicians have begun the practice of Transcendental Meditation and regularly recommend the TM technique to their patients. Dean Ornish, M.D. has demonstrated that heart disease can be reversed with a comprehensive programme that includes meditation. Many physicians consider meditation a key element of an integrated health programme.

The benefits of an ongoing meditation practice as it impacts our health can be classified further into three categories: physiological, psychological, and spiritual. Most people who practice meditation do so to reduce stress, anxiety, anger and other negative emotions. Increasingly, physicians prescribe meditation as part of the treatment for a large and growing number of medical conditions.

Benefits of Meditation

Physical Benefits

- Deep rest—as measured by decreased metabolic rate, lower heart rate, and reduced work load of the heart.

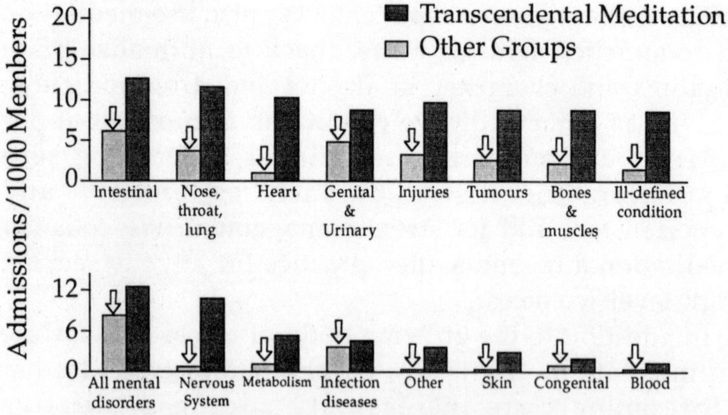

Fig. Reduction in disease incidence among meditators

- Lowered levels of cortisol and lactate-two chemicals associated with stress.
- Reduction of free radicals—unstable oxygen molecules that can cause tissue damage. They are now thought to be a major factor in aging and in many diseases.
- Decreased high blood pressure.
- Higher skin resistance. Low skin resistance is correlated with higher stress and anxiety levels.

- Drop in cholesterol levels. High cholesterol is associated with cardiovascular disease.
- Improved flow of air to the lungs resulting in easier breathing. This has been very helpful to asthma patients.
- Younger biological age. On standard measures of aging, long-term Transcendental Meditation (TM) practitioners (more than five years) measured 12 years younger than their chronological age.
- Higher levels of DHEAS in the elderly. An additional sign of youthfulness through Transcendental Meditation (TM); lower levels of DHEAS are associated with aging.

Psychological Benefits

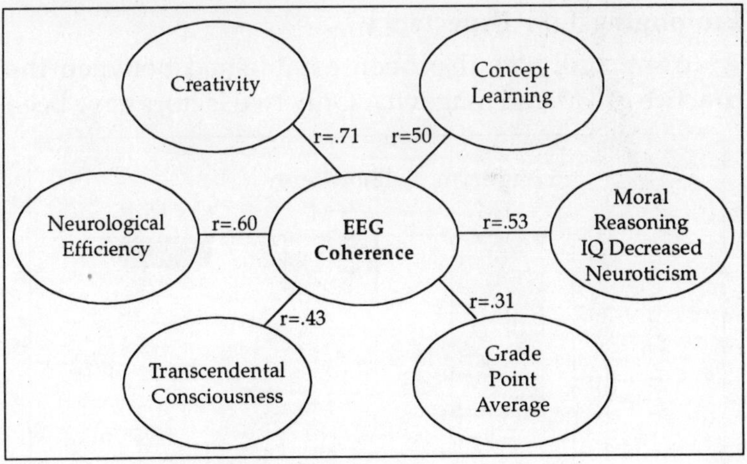

Fig. Psychological benefits of meditation

Increased brain wave coherence. Harmony of brain wave activity in different parts of the brain is associated with greater creativity, improved moral reasoning, and higher IQ.

- Decreased anxiety
- Decreased depression

- Decreased irritability and moodiness
- Improved learning ability and memory
- Increased self-actualization
- Increased feelings of vitality and rejuvenation
- Increased happiness
- Increased emotional stability

Health Conditions that are Benefited by Meditation

Drug Addiction

The Transcendental Meditation technique has proven to be a successful coping strategy in helping to deal with drug addiction, a useful tool in psycho-neuro-immunology (PNI) by helping to control the immune system, and an effective manager of stress and pain.

Prolonging Life Expectancy

A strong link has also been established between the practice of TM and longevity. Only two factors have been

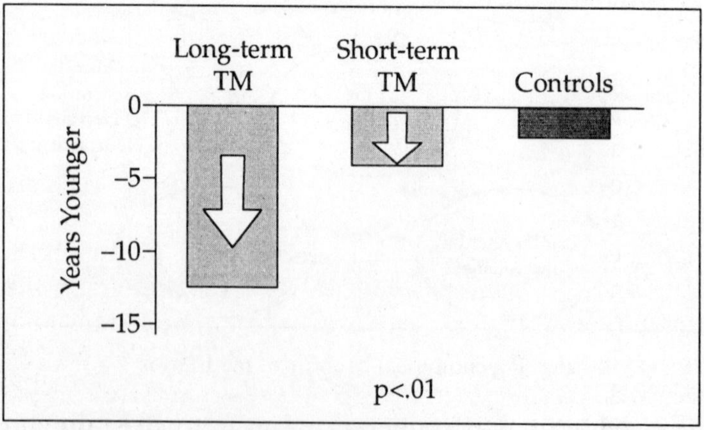

Fig. Age reversal research

scientifically determined to actually extend life: caloric restriction and lowering of the body's core temperature. Meditation has been shown to lower core body temperature.

Stress Control

Most of the people who get on meditation do so because of its beneficial effects on stress. Stress refers to any or all the various pressures experienced in life. These can stem from work, family, illness, or environment and can contribute to such conditions as anxiety, hypertension, and heart disease. How an individual sees things and how he or she handles them makes a big difference in terms of how much stress he or she experiences.

Research has shown that hormones and other biochemical compounds in the blood indicative of stress tend to decrease during meditation practice. These changes also stabilize over time, so that a person is actually less stressed biochemically during daily activity.

This reduction of stress translates directly into a reduction of anxiety and tension. Literally dozens of studies have shown this.

Pain Management

Chronic pain can systematically erode the quality of life. Although great strides are being made in traditional medicine to treat recurring pain, treatment is rarely as simple as prescribing medication or surgery.

Anxiety decreases the threshold for pain and pain causes anxiety. The result is a vicious cycle. Compared with people who feel relaxed, those under stress experience pain more intensely and become even more stressed, which aggravates their pain. Meditation breaks this cycle.

Childbirth preparation classes routinely teach pregnant women deep breathing exercises to minimize the pain and anxiety of labor. Few call it breath meditation, but that's what it is.

Meditative techniques are also a key element in the Arthritis self-help Course at Stanford University. More than 100,000 people with arthritis have taken the

12-hour course and learned meditation-style relaxation exercises as part of a comprehensive self-care program. Graduates report a 15 to 20 per cent reduction in pain.

In one study overseen by Dr. Kabat-Zinn, 72 per cent of the patients with chronic pain conditions achieved at least a 33 per cent reduction after participating in an eight-week period of mindful meditation, while 61-per cent of the pain patients achieved at least a 50 per cent reduction. Additionally, these people perceived their bodies as being 30 per cent less problematic, suggesting an overall improvement in self-esteem and positive views regarding their bodies.

Meditation may not eliminate pain, but it helps people cope more effectively.

Cancer and other Chronic Illness

Meditation and other approaches to deep relaxation help centre people so they can figure out how they'd like to handle the illness and proceed with life. Dr. Ainslie Meares, an Australian psychiatrist who uses meditation with cancer patients, studied seventy-three patients who had attended at least twenty sessions of intensive meditation, and wrote: "Nearly all such patients can expect significant reduction of anxiety and depression, together with much less discomfort and pain. There is reason to expect a 10 per cent chance of quite remarkable slowing of the rate of growth of the tumour, and a 50 per cent chance of greatly improved quality of life."

Heart Disease

Meditation is a key component of Ornish therapy, the only treatment scientifically proven to reverse heart disease.

High Blood Pressure

As soon as Dr. Benson learned that TM reliably reduced blood pressure in meditators, he taught the relaxation response to 36 people with moderately elevated blood pressure. After several weeks of practice, their average blood pressure declined significantly, reducing their risk of stroke and heart attack.

Infertility

Couples dealing with infertility may become depressed, anxious and angry. To help them cope, Alice D. Domar, Ph.D., a psychologist at the Mind / Body Medical Institute, taught the relaxation response to one group of infertile couples. Compared with a similar group of infertile couples who did not learn deep relaxation, the meditators experienced less distress-and were more likely to get pregnant.

Psoriasis

This disease causes scaly red patches on the skin. A pilot study at Dr. Kabat-Zinn's clinic suggests that compared with the skin patches of people with psoriasis who receive only standard medical therapy, the skin patches of those who also meditate clear up more quickly.

Respiratory Crises

Asthma, emphysema and chronic obstructive pulmonary disease (COPD) all restrict breathing and raise fears of suffocation, which in turn makes breathing even more difficult. Studies at Dr. Kabat-Zinn's clinic show that when people with these respiratory conditions learn breath meditation, they have fewer respiratory crises.

Premenstrual Syndrome (PMS), Tension Headaches

Meditation can ease physical complaints such as premenstrual syndrome (PMS), tension headaches and other common health problems.

Meditation gives people a psychological buffer so that life's hectic pace doesn't knock them out. Practicing meditation is like taking a vacation once or twice a day. When you nurture yourself, you accrue tremendous spin-off benefits.

For example, when you are under high stress, it can worsen symptoms of PMS because stress can cause the muscle tension associated with PMS complaints such as fatigue, soreness and aching. On the other hand, when you meditate regularly, you dramatically reduce your body's response to stress, and that can ease the discomfort associated with PMS. The results may not be apparent for several months. You will probably need to meditate regularly for several months before your body responds positively.

Irritable Bowel Syndrome, Ulcers, and Insomnia

Meditation can also improve irritable bowel syndrome, ulcers, and insomnia, among other stress-related conditions. Eighty percent of the people who use meditation to relieve insomnia are successful.

Meditation can help prevent or treat stress-related complaints such as anxiety, headaches and bone, muscle and joint problems. Meditation also provides an inner sense of clarity and calm, and that, in itself, may help ward off certain illnesses.

Fibromyalgia

According to one study, meditation may relieve the discomfort of fibromyalgia, a condition that causes fatigue and intensely painful "trigger points." When 77 men and women with fibromyalgia followed a ten-week stress-reduction program using meditation, all reported that their symptoms improved. And half described their improvements as "moderate to marked."

Psychological Benefits of Meditation

Meditation can help most people feel less anxious and more in control. The awareness that meditation brings can also be a source of personal insight and self-understanding.

Handling Repressed Memories and Enjoying Life

Dr. Borysenko notes that "meditation may lead to a breakdown of screen memories so that early childhood abuse episodes and other traumas suddenly flood the mind, making the patient temporarily more anxious until these traumas are healed. Many so-called meditation exercises are actually forms of imagery and visualization that are extraordinarily useful in healing old traumas, confronting death anxieties, finishing 'old business', learning to forgive, and enhancing self-esteem."

"Meditation frees persons from tenacious preoccupation with the past and future and allows them to fully experience life's precious moments", says Daeja Napier, founder of the Insight Meditation Center and lay dharma teacher of insight meditation in suburban Boston.

"Many men and women tend to live in a state of perpetual motion and expectation that prevents them from appreciating the gifts that each moment gives us," says Napier. "We live life in a state of insufficiency, waiting for a mother to love us, for a father to be kind to us, for the perfect job or home, for Prince Charming to come along or to become a perfect person. It's a mythology that keeps us from being whole.

"Meditation is a humble process that gently returns us to the now of our lives and allows us to wake up and re-evaluate the way that we live our lives," says Napier. "We realize that the only thing missing is mindfulness, and that's what we practice."

Depression

Feelings of helplessness, hopelessness and isolation are hallmarks of depression—the nation's most prevalent mental health problem. Meditation increases self-confidence and feelings of connection to others. Many studies have shown that depressed people feel much better after eliciting the relaxation response.

Panic Attacks

Sometimes anxiety becomes paralyzing and people feel (wrongly) that they are about to suffer some horrible fate. Panic attacks are often treated with drugs, but studies by Jon Kabat-Zinn, Ph.D., associate professor of medicine at the University of Massachusetts Medical Center in Worcester and director of the medical center's Stress Reduction Clinic, show that if people who are prone to panic attacks begin focused, meditative breathing the instant they feel the first signs of an episode, they are less likely to have a full-blown panic attack.

Spiritual Benefits of Meditation

The longer an individual practices meditation, the greater the likelihood that his or her goals and efforts will shift toward personal and spiritual growth. Many individuals who initially learn meditation for its self-regulatory aspects find that as their practice deepens they are drawn more and more into the realm of the "spiritual."

In her work with many cancer and AIDS patients, Dr. Borysenko has observed that many are most interested in meditation as a way of becoming more attuned to the spiritual dimension of life. She reports that many die "healed," in a state of compassionate self-awareness and self-acceptance.

Illness in general

"It doesn't seem to matter what type of medical condition brings people to the Stress Reduction Clinic," Dr. Kabat-Zinn observes. "Over the eight-week programme, they usually report a reduction in symptoms."

Glossary

Abhyantara vrtti	:	inhalation
Anuloma ujjayi	:	breathing in through the mouth and out through nostril
Apana-vayu	:	air in the lower abdomen
Asat	:	non-being
Ayama	:	expansion or extension
Bahya vrtti	:	exhalation
Bandha	:	bond
Bhastrika	:	bellows or forced rapid deep breathing
Bhramari	:	nasal vibration of palate
Chakra	:	an energy centre in the body
Citta	:	consciousness
Jalandhara bandha	:	chin lock
Kapalabhati	:	cleansing breath
Kevala kumbaka	:	perfectly peaceful pause
Kumbhaka	:	pause after inhalation or exhalation
Plavini	:	air-swallowing
Prana	:	cosmic energy which is self-energising
Prana-vayu	:	air in the chest
Pranayama	:	yogic breathing exercises
Puruka	:	single inhalation
Rechaka	:	exhalation
Sahasara	:	thousand-petalled lotus
Samana-vayu	:	air in the body
Sat	:	being

Sitali	tongue hissing or sound made by drawing in air through protruding tongue folded into a tube
Sitkali	teeth hissing or noise made by drawing air through the front teeth
Stambha vrtti	breath retention
Udana-vayu	air in the throat
Uddiyana bandha	raising the diaphragm
Ujjayi	pranayama technique of contracting vocal chords
Viloma ujjayi	breathing in through one nostril and out through the mouth
Vyana-vayu	air throughout the body.

Index